A Gangster's Revenge II

Lock Down Publications
Presents
A Gangster's Revenge II
A Novel by *Aryanna*

Lock Down Publications
P.O. Box 1482
Pine Lake, Ga 30072-1482

Visit our website at www.lockdownpublications.com

First Edition October 2015
Printed in the United States of America

This is a work of fiction. Names, characters, places, and incidents either are products of the author's imagination or are used fictitiously. Any similarity to actual events or locales or persons, living or dead, is entirely coincidental.

Lock Down Publications
Like our page on Facebook: Lock Down Publications @www.facebook.com/lockdownpublications.ldp
Cover design and layout by: Jamie Lee
Book interior design by: Shawn Walker
Edited by: Lauren Burton

ACKNOWLEDGMENTS

As always, my thanks goes to God first because there is no me without his blessings. I have to thank my fans because you motivated me to come back with a vengeance, your support means the world to me! I have to thank part of the amazing team behind me KID DOODLE, IZZY and my beautiful BELINDA. I LOVE YOU ALL and couldn't do it without you. You're the foundation of STREET DREAMERZ ENTERTAINMENT. But we are a family above anything else.

I have to thank my god mother, MONICA, because you have been in my corner since day one. I'm happy I have made you proud but I CAN'T LET OFF THE GAS NOW LOL!

I have to thank everyone who believes in me as well as those who continue to doubt me, either way you motivate me. I most definitely have to thank the other part of my amazing team, my LDP family your love and support have been invaluable to me but know that I'm going to give it all back. LDP, we in here and The Game Is Ours!

I got to thank my brother from another mother, MILWAUKEE "DA PIMP", for his eyes and ears during the creative process. GET THERE MAN!

Last, but never the least, I have to thank my precious, ARYANNA. I do it for you, baby girl, and I'm forever thankful that you changed my life.

DEDICATION

This book is dedicated to the little people that's inside of us all, that have the courage to dream.

Aryanna

Chapter One

2027

Candy

The gunshots jerked my body upright, coming so close together they sounded like one, leaving them breathless. My mind played tricks on me as I watched two scenes unfold before me: one full of blood, agony, and screams versus the eerily calm one where the moonlight glistened off the chrome .45 outstretched in my steady hand. The shaking would come later. It always did.

"The dream?" she asked, gently taking the gun from my hand and sliding it back under my pillow.

"The nightmare."

"Want to talk about it?"

"What's left to say?"

"I wasn't there, so I don't know. But I'd like to."

"You want me to tell you how he was shot? Again? Why? Why do you want me to torture both of us with those details?"

"You keep so much bottled in. You carry that impossible burden every single day. I know how much that hurts. I loved him, too."

In those late night hours at the height of that gray area between today and tomorrow was the only time we could give a voice to our pain, our loss. It was then that I could allow myself to feel something other than revenge, other than the raw razor-sharp, a devastation, and really greedy for all I'd lost.

Shaking started, and she pulled me slowly to her, but still I held onto the images in my mind. I needed to see them, needed to remember that which drove me every day so the yesterdays of my life couldn't be filled with excuses. I needed the pain. Without it, I would die. "Whew. I don't wanna talk about it,

Mona. I can't. All I can do is remember and wish to God that we done things differently."

"Shh. Baby, how could you do it differently? You loved him and he loved you, just like I did. No one saw it coming. But come here," she whispered, taking my face in her hands and kissing me softly, yet urgently.

My body reacted immediately as it always did when it came to her. His Mona. My Mona, too. I let her push me back against the pillows, enjoying the sweetness of her kisses while her fingers glided over the familiar curves of my body. She knew the landscape almost better than her own body. Slipping two fingers inside me, she bit my bottom lip gently. I was so wet. I could hear my pussy talking to her while she played the sweet melody inside me, using her thumb to rub my clit just the way I liked it. My back arched when she hit my spots, and her name tumbled from my mouth on a sweet side of needed satisfaction.

Still working her magic with her fingers, she let her lips and tongue roam my body freely, sucking my sensitive nipples until they hurt so good that all I could do was whimper. Pulling on her mass of black curls, I guided her head lower, needing to feel the release that only she could bring.

The fingers were replaced by her tongue, and my world shook.

"Mona!"

"I gotchu, baby. Just enjoy the ride."

"Oh shit. Oh shit. Mmm. Shit!"

She tortured me, licking slow, lazy circles one minute and nibbling on my clit the next. Trying to run did me no good. She devoured me until my screams rang out loud and clear, passion shattering the stillness of the night.

"Mona, Mona, Mona," I chanted, coming so hard I thought I might pull her hair out at the roots. I lay there covered in sweat, willing my heart not to burst out of my chest while she sat back with a satisfied grin and reached for a blunt.

"You! You think that shit's funny, huh?"

Her laughter was answer enough, and I couldn't help smiling while taking the lit blunt from her and filling my lungs with its potent smoke. If I was going to be honest, I did have to admit I loved the way she worked my body, how she knew exactly what to do without even a hint of suggestion. Only two other people had known my body so well. And I couldn't wait to kill one of them.

"You're thinking about him again."

There was no point in denying it. It was actually rare that my thoughts weren't on him. My love. My lover. Her husband.

I hit the blunt two more times and passed it to her before getting out of the bed, grabbing a cigarette, and walking to the window. I didn't light it at first. I simply stood there and watched the horizon take on the color of hot coals as the sun began its climb, wondering how many times he'd stood in that exact spot looking at that exact site.

I felt her eyes on me, felt her love and compassion without her having to lift a finger to give me either one. She gave me hope. For five long years we battled the streets hand-in-hand, sometimes back-to-back, but our toughest fights came against the unseen demons that lurked in the night and preyed on the soul's vulnerabilities. Still we stood, our scars plainly visible to one another, but hidden from all other eyes that might not understand how our union came to be. We understood, we endured, and we loved each other as much as our broken hearts would allow.

Turning to the dresser, I picked up the lighter – his lighter – and lit my cigarette.

"Candy?"

"Hmm?"

"I know."

Those two words said so much, but more than words was the actual knowledge that she did know and understood. Walking back to the bed, I studied her naked body, appraising it lovingly, knowing she could feel my touch with only my eyes being on her. I took the blunt from her, putting it in the ashtray with the still-smoldering cigarette, and pulled her to the middle of the bed. Starting with her delicate feet, I kissed my way up her body, letting her breathing speak to me the way lovers do and guide me on the familiar adventure of her wants and needs.

She smelled like honey and tasted like that last bite of chocolate mama said not to eat for dinner. Upward I worked until I reached the silky curls that danced with every exhale of my breath, giving me a glimpse at her beautiful pink and oh-so-sweet pussy.

"Candy Cane," she panted as I took my first lick of her sweet treasure.

I drank greedily from her well in equal measures of give and take, teasing her as she did me.

"Oh fuck! Candy, don't. Fuck!" she moaned when I pushed her legs up, spread her firm ass cheeks, and let my tongue glide across her asshole like a gentle breeze. I played tag, alternating between ass and pussy, nibbling, sucking, biting, and licking. Finally, I gave her what I knew she wanted, inserting one finger in her ass and two more inside her throbbing pussy, working all of them at a steady rhythm until she almost levitated with her orgasmic shock. Her nails pierced my skin as she grabbed onto me, using me as the anchor as she rode the wave of her climax to its end.

We stayed locked in an embrace, her holding me gently, stroking my back so softly it gave me goose bumps. I could hear her heart beating steadily and feel the sweat running freely down the valley between her succulent breasts. I marveled at the fact that I even loved the smell of her sweat. What I loved most was that she knew me through both good and bad, and that knowledge proved she still loved me.

Knowledge of understanding and forgiveness pushed the words from my mouth as tears clouded my vision and the past became the present. "Kiara had been acting funny ever since she'd come back from the doctors. It wasn't like she said anything. It was the silence that spoke for her. We never lacked for conversation, but that night it was like pulling teeth to get her to say anything. I knew something was wrong. I didn't know if she found out I was pregnant or that me and Devaughn had sex that day."

I felt her arms tight around me, loving, urging me to go on.

"I heard when you all got home, but when I got up to go downstairs, the look in her eyes froze me in place. I've never seen love and hate war so hard in the same body before, and I was halfway expecting the sizzle of electricity followed by a clap of thunder. I ain't no bitch, but I shivered when she looked at me. She asked me if I loved her, and I told her yes. She asked me if I loved her more than I loved him. I tried to answer, even willing to lie only to avoid hurting her, but the words wouldn't come. She just walked out of the room, and I followed behind her like the disloyal bitch I was. In my wildest dreams, I never thought she'd hurt him. I mean, this was her favorite brother. Didn't you love beyond reason? Way beyond reason."

I took a deep breath and extracted myself from her warm embrace, reaching for and relighting the blunt before I lay back down beside her. The rising sun looked like it was underwater. My tear-stained vision shimmered and shifted until I had to close my eyes against it. He loved sunrises.

I felt her hand on mine as she laced our fingers together. She'd wait forever if I needed her to, which was just one more reason why I loved her. I took a deep pull on the blunt and let the smoke scorch my lungs, not feeling any pain. No pain compared to what I'd been through.

"The first chance I got, I pulled him to the side and told him that I thought she found out about that morning. He asked how, and when I told him about Tara, he sent Deshana. He could tell something was wrong, too, but not just wrong. Off. Kiara was pistol-whipping Skino mercilessly. I mean, I ain't never seen her snap like that. Her getting her hands dirty was the first thing that was wrong, but the lack of emotion, that's what made it *off*. Deshana came back with her hands bloody. We knew that she knew. Still, we thought at the most it was gonna be an argument. Nobody thought…"Devaughn killed Skino, and that's when shit got ill. Kiara confronted him about us still fucking, and before I knew what was happening, she slapped me. Took my gun and had one pointed at me while the other was pointed at him. Time stopped. All I could think about was our baby. I wanted to save our baby."

I felt her fingers tighten on mine a little and my heart broke some more for her. I knew it bothered her that she couldn't give her husband a baby – a baby that we had. I couldn't speak to his pain because deep down I couldn't relate to it, and to try would be like spitting in her face.

I handed her the blunt, lit another cigarette, and continued. "She took everyone by surprise, but she had so many tricks up her sleeve that I don't think any of us could get a grasp on reality. She knew we were fucking, she knew I was pregnant. But you could still feel the suspense building. When she said she was pregnant, I was surprised just like everyone else, but when she said it was his, I was fucked up! It had to be a lie. He wouldn't fuck his own sister, and I knew that. What I didn't know, what nobody knew, was that she would fuck him. She told him how she snuck into his room while he was passed out and fucked him until he came and passed back out. Anybody other than Dee and

I would have said that he knew who he was fucking, but not with all those girls we had in the house then. She fucked him. In every way possible, she fucked him. And the twisted part is that she was as much in love with him as we were. They didn't grow up together, and she didn't want him to be her brother. She wanted it all!"

The swift-building anger checked my tears, making me wish I could wrap my hands around the gun under my pillow and squeeze bullet after bullet into someone's face. Not just anyone's face. Her face! "The look on Dee's face said it all. He understood even before she said anything that he would have to choose. How could he? Despite everything she'd done, she was carrying his unborn child and he couldn't make that child pay for that mistake. He wouldn't. I begged him, and the last thing he said was my name. To this day that haunts me."

Aryanna

Chapter Two

I smoked the last of the cigarette, put it out, and lit another one. Still she held my hand and said nothing, simply staring at the room she used to share with him. I didn't know what she saw, what memories they made, but I didn't envy her them. Every day I had a new memory of him to add to my collection, and I knew God blessed me with that gift.

"She shot him," I said softly, knowing the echo of those three words was the loudest thing either of us had ever heard. I passed her the cigarette and grabbed the .45 from its resting place, loving the familiar feel of its cold metal in my hand. It used to be his gun, and one day it would avenge what happened to him. "He fired off a wild shot that hit her in the arm, causing her to drop the gun she had pointed at me. I was too stunned to grab it, though. I just sat there and cried, holding my stomach while Deshana ran to him. So much blood. I couldn't. He'd almost died in my arms once. I couldn't go through that again.

"I never did figure out how the doctors got there or who called them, but I'm guessing it was her. When they rushed in was when I noticed she was gone. I'm not sure how much time passed, but I knew. I knew. They pronounced him, and that's when I blacked out. I guess it was more like I blanked out, because when my mind started working again, I was curled up on the floor of the library. You know the rest," I concluded, gently stroking the pistol with a loving mother's touch.

We both sat in comfortable silence as the day began all around us, both of us still stuck in the tragedy of five years ago. I never knew what she was thinking at times like this because she always did the same thing after I told her what happened: she went inside herself.

Losing her husband had changed her more than any of us. I'd adjusted my life accordingly. Deshana had gone off to college on the west coast, needing to distance herself from here. Day-Day and Latavia had both finished college and now had respectable careers in music and law. Of course, things changed for everybody. From what I had heard, even little Jordyn had taken it hard.

But nobody had changed like Ramona. She quit being a probation officer and joined her family's business. "This thing of ours" is what she called it. I called it the mob. She'd given up her straight-laced life where she hadn't even had a parking ticket and embraced the criminal world like a long-lost love. The scary part was that she was good at it. Really good at it. Within the first year she had taken over half of Kiara's operations in Virginia, legal and illegal, hoping it would bring her out of hiding. She was a corporate woman by day and a criminal queen by night. Nothing scared her, not even the law. After all, Devaughn's oldest daughter, Latavia, was one hell of a lawyer.

She even managed to take Kiara's house from her, at least the one that we still lived in. It felt right to stay here with him all around us. It was all we had.

She put her cigarette out and, still holding my hand, laid her head on my chest. I gathered the covers around us and held on to her as our thoughts took us off to a sleep we prayed didn't have dreams at its end.

The sound of my name being called woke me up several hours later.

"Mama? Mama? Mama, wake up."

"What is it, Junior?"

"I'm hungry."

"Okay, so why don't you tell the cook to make you breakfast?"

"Because."

"Because what, DJ?"

"Because I want you to do it. And because I wanna see my daddy."

I'd already pretty much figured out that was at the heart of the situation. I'd actually thought he would've made this request yesterday since he never missed more than two days, but I didn't consider the fact he hadn't been feeling well.

"Okay, I'm coming. Go get dressed."

He leapt onto the bed, knocking the pistol to the floor, and gave me and Ramona hugs and kisses. After he succeeded in making both of us laugh, he got down off the bed, picked up the gun, and handed it to me.

"Don't lose Daddy's gun, Ma. He's gonna want it back." With that, he took off back to his room.

He looked so much like his father it made me want to smile and cry at the same time.

"He looks just like him," Ramona said, voicing my thoughts.

"The only difference in the two is DJ's dreads. I kind of figured he'd want him to have them, though."

She nodded her head thoughtfully before turning to look at me. "I have to go out of town."

"When?"

"Today."

"Where?"

"Italy."

"Huh? Like the country?"

"You know another Italy?"

"Not other than the strip club. Can you tell me why?" We didn't really have secrets, but I wasn't a part of that thing of hers, so I normally didn't ask. Her having to go all the way home was serious, though.

"It's business, but don't worry. I haven't done anything wrong. I shouldn't be more than a few days, and you know I'm gonna call you."

"Are you taking the GV?"

"No, I'm not taking anyone with me, so I'm only taking the G III. Don't give me that look, my father asked to see me, and I'm not about to disrespect him by showing up with guards. What do I have to fear? Besides, the guards will be here for you and DJ."

I wanted to argue, but I wouldn't. "Just be careful."

Her response was a kiss, slow and sweet and full of love. It was a promise.

"I love you, Mona."

"I love you too, Candy. How about we take a quick shower and you let me show you just how much?"

I could feel my body heat up as she touched me there again, but I had my own things to take care of. "What time do you leave?"

"4:00 p.m."

"I'm sorry, baby, but it will have to wait until you come back."

"DJ?"

"Uh-huh."

"Then I'll just have to make sure I hurry back to you, huh?"

"You better," I said, kissing her again and touching her where she touched me. Before I knew it, we were both panting as we each played our own song to the beat of a simultaneous climax. I felt her cum gush onto my hand as I'm sure she felt mine do to her. I slowly licked my fingers, never taking my eyes off her while she did the same. Then we shared the sweetest, softest rainbow kiss, and I tasted both of us on my tongue.

"Mm, you make me never want to leave."

"I know the feeling. You gotta go, though. We don't need him coming to look for you."

"I know. What are you gonna do?"

"I'm gonna take our son to see his dad, then I'm gonna go to the gun range."

"You don't need the practice."

"Trust me, I wanna be able to hit that bitch from a thousand yards if I have to."

Aryanna

Chapter Three

Keyz

"Devonte, come get these damn toys out of the middle of my floor!"

"Okay."

"Now, Devonte!"

"I'm coming, Mommy." And sure enough his slender frame bent the corner, walking with that same arrogance his father had. Must be genetic. That wasn't the only thing he'd inherited, though. He had the smile, the eyes, and I'd even witnessed how all the little girls flocked to him, so he definitely had the charm. He was only five, but he was gonna be a heartbreaker, just like his father.

The looming anniversary of his death had me thinking about him more than usual, every second instead of every other one. I loved and I hated him. Not in equal measure, not anymore. I loved him more every day in part because of the amazing little boy he'd given me, but mostly because I'd loved him all my life and there was no stopping that shit. But even the grave came between it.

And the hate. The hate was why I'd killed him. I hated the fact that I couldn't have him like I wanted to because it wasn't *politically correct*. We didn't have to deal with society's rules. Who the fuck were they to judge us? But he hadn't wanted me anyway. He wanted her.

It didn't matter now, though, because none of us had him. I still had my little boy, though, and he was perfect. Even when he pissed me off.

"Come here, Tay," I told him, picking him up and sitting on the couch with him. "I'm sorry I yelled at you, but you know better, right?"

"Yes, ma'am."

"So we're good?" I asked, sticking out my pinkie toward him. He locked his tiny pinkie with mine and gave me the smile that always made my heart beat harder. "Who's your favorite Mommy?"

"You're my only Mommy," he replied, laughing.

I loved his laugh. It was my laugh, but I knew when he got older it would take on a deep, richer tone like his father's. How I wished his father could see him or talk to him and see how intelligent he was for a five year old.

"What's wrong?"

"Nothing, baby."

"Then why are your eyes watering?"

"Because I'm about to sneeze all over you," I said, tickling him until he squirmed away from me. Normally I would chase him, but today I just didn't feel up to it. "Listen, Tay, I want you to go get dressed because your aunt is coming to pick you up soon."

"Which aunt?" he asked

"Your Aunt Vita."

I could see his little mind working with this information, trying to figure out where he was going. Vita was actually Victoria, my on-again, off-again girlfriend whom I'd been with for almost two years. We were mostly on, but I couldn't commit to her. I still had trust issues after what happened with Candy. I did trust her, though, or else I wouldn't let her within a hundred feet of my little prince. He was all I had left.

"Where we going?" Tay asked excitedly

"You are going to Madison Square Garden to see the Knicks play."

"Who are they playing?"

Now, you would think he'd be too excited to ask a question like that, but I guess that shows how spoiled he was. Shit, he went to the Garden all the time. The only person more recognizable than him was Spike Lee. He was my baby, my only child. I had every intention of giving him the world.

"They're playing Boston."

His mind was working a mile a minute. "Hmm, tough choice, but I'm going to have to wear my Knicks jersey," he said, walking toward his room.

I smiled. That was my little man. Following him down the hall, I went into my own bedroom and stripped out of the sweats I had on. I had a meeting, and that required a professional touch.

Naked now, I walked into my closet and picked out a black Gucci cocktail dress and some four-inch stilettos to match. I grabbed a matching red bra and thong set out of my dresser, laid everything on my bed, and went to start my bubble bath. Putting in the bath salts that kept my honey-colored skin baby bottom soft, I turned on the Jacuzzi jets and put on my slow jams CD. With that my sanctuary was complete, except for the blunt I needed.

Walking back into the room, I noticed Mark's eyes on me, but I didn't pay him any attention. I rolled my blunt on autopilot, my thoughts going back to where my heart was: Devaughn. I hadn't visited his grave, but maybe it was time I did, at least for our son's sake.

"Kiara?" Mark called my name.

"What did you call me?" I asked, snapping my head in his direction, wishing for my gun to appear in my hand at that moment.

"Damn, ma, chill. I called you like five times, but you ain't say shit."

"My name is Keyz. Don't disrespect me by calling me anything else, understand?"

"Yeah, a'ight, ma. Just come here and let me talk to you right fast."

That was his lame attempt at code for he wanted to fuck. I shook my head, more disgusted with myself than angry at him, because after a whole year I still couldn't figure out why I was with this nigga. I could fuck any nigga I wanted to, gay or otherwise. I was a bad bitch, hands down, so why him?

Knowing the answer didn't help, it just made me more disgusted with myself. He reminded me of the love I lost. Reminded me of him. I had everything any woman would ever need houses around the world, money, power, and respect. My son, my health, and my freedom, but I didn't have him. I had what I needed, but I didn't have what I wanted most, what I'd sacrificed a normal life for. What I wouldn't give to have him back, if only for a little while, if only to hear all he'd had to say.

Grabbing my lighter, I lit my blunt and stood in front of my floor-to-ceiling window overlooking the Hudson. I wasn't worried about someone seeing me: one because I was in the penthouse and I owned the entire building, and two because I really didn't give a fuck. I heard the water stop, alerting me to my full tub that waited while the classic harmonies of Mr. Vandross floated effortlessly to my ears, wrapping me in their embrace.

I still felt his eyes on me, felt their hunger, and as much as I hated it, I felt my body react on its own in the form of the sudden wetness between my legs. I took a deep breath and hit my blunt, thinking maybe a line of coke would put my mind at ease. Luther's music was soothing, but my soul was restless. I knew what I needed, what would release some of this pressure I felt on my chest. The time had come.

I heard him moving around behind me, and the soft click as he closed the door and locked it. Only seconds passed before I felt his hands on my hips, his lips on my neck, and his dick poking me not so softly on the ass. Still I kept my eyes on the river, slowly smoking and letting my mind run through options until one slid into place and fit snugly. For the first time, I smiled.

Taking that as his cue, he bent me over gently and pushed inside my warm wetness in a deliberately slow motion. I couldn't deny the feeling building within me, and when he pulled back for his second stroke, I threw my beautiful ass back at him, loving the moan that came from somewhere deep inside him. I tried to be cute and hit the blunt while he hit it, but by his fifth stroke I knew he was trying to push up into my rib cage and all thought of anything else had escaped his mind. I wanted to protest when he grabbed my hair, but my first orgasm reduced me to unintelligible moans.

"Damn, you feel so good, ma. Shit, I'm about to. 'Bout to."

I knew I should have let him get his, too, but before he could I stopped him by standing straight up and turning around to face him.

"What the fuck, boo? Why you stop?" He complained.

"Shh, lay on the bed."

"Oh, you gonna ride me, huh?"

"Eat me first," I said, squatting over his face, leaving him no choice but to eat me. Grabbing two handfuls of my ass, he pulled me all the way to him until I thought he might suffocate in my pussy. What he lacked in skill he more than made up for with enthusiasm, sucking on my clit so hard I thought it might come off in his mouth. It felt good, though.

It wasn't him that was sampling the flavors of my kitty-cat, though. In my mind I was reliving the night I rode Devaughn until he screamed. "Mm. That's it right there. Eat this good pussy. Umm. Oh. Oh, fuck!" I felt my earth moving again, and in the blink of an eye I'd slipped down his chest, taken ahold of his dick, and put it back in me. My pussy was hot and throbbing, my juices were flowing, and I saw his eyes glaze over with renewed hunger. Grabbing his shoulders, I rode him hard and fast, desperate to free myself and dive off the cliff of fulfillment. "I'm. I'm. Dee!" I screamed, cumming in great waves of orgasmic bliss.

It only took a second to realize that he wasn't moving under me, although he was still rock hard and very much buried inside me.

"What did you say? Bitch, I know you ain't just call me another nigga's name!" His face was twisted in anger.

The truth was I had. The shocking part was I'd done it on purpose. Climbing off him, I hurried into my closet and threw the lid off the only pair of Jordans in there reaching my hand in without bothering to look.

"Bitch, do you hear me?" he yelled.

Yeah, I heard him. When I walked back into the room, he was standing in the middle of my bedroom floor, dick swinging and too pissed to care. It was almost funny. Almost.

"I told you never to call me out of my name," I replied, using all my strength to keep my emotions under control.

"Fuck you! You just called me some other nigga's name while we were fucking! You lucky I ain't punch you in your muthafuckin' face, you trick-ass bitch. I don't know how they do it in VA, but this New York here, ma!"

"Trick-ass bitch?" He made this easy for me. Then again, all he did was act like any man would with a bruised ego.

"You heard what I said. Yo, I don't need this shit. Go fuck that nigga since you want him so bad. Pussy ain't no good, anyway!"

I laughed at that. "No good, huh?"

"I've had better."

"Stop lying on your dick, you nothing-ass nigga. You ain't neva had better. And you never will."

The look on his face said he meant to hit me when he took his first step, until he saw the gun I've been hiding behind my back.

"What's up, slim? You look like you wanted to hit me, so why you stop? Don't let this little piece of metal stop you. What's popping?"

"You ain't even worth it. I'm done with your ass."

"Indeed."

There was a knock on the door. "Mommy, I'm ready and Auntie Vita is here."

"Okay. I'll be out in a minute, little man."

"'Kay."

I'm wasn't sure why Mark was smiling, but it annoyed me. "What you smiling for?"

"Because you ain't gonna kill me with your son and your girl in the house, bitch!"

I smiled a smile that I knew wouldn't reach my hazel eyes. What did he think the silencer was for? I shot him three times in the chest, admiring the nice, clean holes my 9mm Beretta put in him.

Funny, he wasn't smiling anymore.

Sitting the gun on the dresser, I retrieved and relit my blunt from earlier, taking it into the bathroom with me. I smoked and soaked in the tub for half an hour. I was feeling good and finally relaxed. It always helped to murder someone.

The cleanup wouldn't be a problem since the whole house had black marble floors, but maybe it was time to redecorate anyway. The penthouse was 4000 square feet with seven bedrooms and four bathrooms, by all means spacious for me and Devonte. It was comfortable and homey. Nah, no need to change any of that.

Stepping out of the tub, I got lotioned up, perfumed down, and dressed quickly. Ordinarily I'd never wear my hair in a ponytail, but fucking with my micro braids wasn't an option right now. Slipping on my stilettos, I stepped over Mark's body once again, opened my door, and made my way to the living room.

I could hear cartoons on the eighty-inch plasma and Vita laughing right along with Devonte. I loved his laugh. I walked into the living room to find him huddled up on the couch watching Scooby Doo, the crazy, lovable dog he was. They were so good together, and I knew Vita loved him almost as much as I did. I was beginning to think that if anything happened to me, I'd want my precious baby boy to be with her.

I didn't want him growing up in my world if he didn't have to, and I had enough money to make sure he didn't have to. Who knew what path he'd choose when the time came, though. His mama and his daddy were both gangstas. Did he really have a chance?

I'd use my last breath to make sure he did.

"What's up, Vita?"

"Hey," she replied in a standoffish tone. That only meant one thing, she knew Mark was here. Did I have a surprise for her!

"Vita, let me holler at you for a minute," I said, walking back toward my bedroom, knowing curiosity would make her follow me despite her attitude. When she got to the door she looked at the dead body, looked at me, then looked back at the body. She said nothing, simply giving me that questioning look that said, *what the fuck?*

"It's not even important, and that's not what I want to talk to you about. I've got a meeting to go to and it's a big deal. I got a pretty good idea what it's about, but there's nothing I can do about it now except go."

"Blood business?"

"More or less. I want you to keep Tay until you hear from me. It may be a couple of days, it may be a couple of weeks. Either way, you're the only person I can trust with his life."

The tears in her eyes were plain to see, just like her love. "Is everything going to be alright, K?"

"Yeah. I've just been neglecting a lot of things and putting my responsibilities off. I know what I have to do."

"Just be safe. Please."

"Don't worry, and if shit does go wrong, you and Devonte are straight. My lawyer knows what to do. Now stop looking at me like that and come give me a kiss so I can go."

She hugged me tightly and kissed me with a desperation I'd never felt from her. Our tongues battled like angry lovers, but quickly made up, as we were known to do. Her lips were soft and juicy, almost as full as my own, and she tasted exotic.

I released her and looked her directly in the eyes. "You take care of him and keep him away from this bullshit. He's better than that."

"I know. So are you," she whispered softly.

"Alright, time to go," I said, grabbing my gun off the dresser, slipping it into my purse, and heading for the door.

"What about Mark?"

"I'll have someone clean it up. You just go enjoy the game, okay?"

"Yeah, right. I'll be thinking about you in that sexy-ass black dress all night."

I licked my lips slowly and walked back into the living room to find my son in the same spot. "A'ight, Tay, time to go."

"Mom, why you not coming?"

"Because I got some business I need to take care of. Is that okay with you?"

He looked at me for a while, doing that thinking thing again. Even at his age he was a master at silences and keeping his thoughts closely guarded. "You look pretty."

"Thank you, baby."

He climbed down off the couch and gave me a hug, holding on for a while without saying anything. "I love you, Mama."

"I love you too, baby." People said women had the best intuition, but I swear sometimes I thought kids had us beat. My little boy knew something wasn't as it should be, maybe because it was a rarity that we did anything not together, or maybe he simply knew me well enough even at that age.

Without another word, he let go of me, grabbed Vita's waiting hand, and let her lead him out to the elevator. I thought he might be crying, but he looked back at me before the door closed and gave me that big smile. His Daddy's smile.

Chapter Four

I knew I was smiling back, but now I wanted to cry.

Picking up my cell phone, I pressed a few buttons and listened to it ring on the other end. "It's me. Send someone up here to clean up and bring my car around." I didn't need to wait on a response.

Walking to the elevator, I called another number and waited what seemed like forever for someone to pick up.

"Peace, Blood."

"Peace, Almighty."

"What up, bitch?" she yelled in excitement, recognizing my voice.

I laughed at her crazy-ass, my sister-in-arms whom I hadn't seen in so long I forgot what she looked like. "What's up with you, bitch?"

"Damn, Keyz, I thought you fucking died or some shit! I ain't heard from you in forever."

"Naw, not dead, just on maternity leave. You know how that goes."

"How old is the baby?"

"He's five."

"Five months?"

"Five years old."

"You've been on maternity leave for five years, Keyz?"

"Uh-huh."

"Huh. I'ma take a wild guess that this call is about the meeting." Noodles was the secretary to the council. She was who you had to go through in order to communicate with them. Sure, they could send messages or orders, but you couldn't get word to them except through her.

"Yeah, I need to know where."

"Is your phone secure?"

"Noodles, I haven't forgotten anything, so please don't insult me with trivial shit that's in the Banging 101 handbook."

"Still feisty, huh? You're right, you're a big girl. The Plaza, Suite 1020."

Before I could say anything else, she hung up the phone and the elevator opened into the lobby. Quickly I made my way out to the sleek 800i BMW idling at the curb, giving my destination to the driver holding my door. I folded into the confines of the car, loving the feel and smell of the caramel-colored leather interior almost as to fit my needs, right down to the bulletproof alloy inside my tires and the TVs that were programmed with Devonte's favorite movies, jet black with red rims and diplomatic plates that read "BBA". It was pulled by 800 hp of mean, and it definitely looked the part.

It was impossible to see me inside rolling a blunt laced with a generous gram of cocaine as we glided through Manhattan, but I still put up the privacy partition separating me from the two men in the front. I needed a few moments to myself to get my thoughts in order before I walked inside the lion's den.

Five years ago I wouldn't have been worried about this meeting. I would've just been honored and humbled to receive an invite.

Five years ago he would've been sitting next to me smoking a blunt without the coke.

I lit up and inhaled mightily, looking out at a city I really didn't see and that I'd never really seen despite how long I'd lived here. Five years ago.

I shook my head to get my thoughts focused on the present. No one in the organization knew that I'd killed him, and the story I told was that Skino had managed to do it right before I killed him. Who was alive to challenge me? Overnight I was promoted to five-star general and given all the territory that would've been Devaughn's had he lived. I'd been more or less given the keys to the kingdom and put in the position to one day sit at the roundtable I'd only heard stories about.

I was making history, but after he was gone none of it mattered. Not the money, not the power, not even the respect. I would have traded it all in a heartbeat. In a lot of ways I had, because my focus from the moment I lost him was exclusively on our son. Nothing and no one came before him, and that still wouldn't change, but I understood that the period of mourning I'd been given was over. No one could comprehend what I'd lost, but they somehow believed time would heal all wounds. Not these wounds. Not this time.

I put my blunt out as we pulled up in front of the hotel and let the window back down. "Put extra people on my son at the garden and wait here in the car. I shouldn't be long."

"Extra people? There are already twenty heavily-armed men with him and Vita."

I didn't say one word, just stared him down wondering if he understood that I could kill him as easily as I would light a cigarette.

"I'm sorry, Miss Keyz, I won't question you again."

He quickly exited the car and held my door open for me, so close I could feel the fear on him. He wasn't a pussy to be scared of me. He was smart.

One thing I had managed to do was cultivate a lot of new legitimate business in New York since my arrival, including building a lucrative security firm that protected anybody for the right price. I had a very loyal and very deadly team separate from my organization, which made me smart and not simply paranoid.

I walked into the hotel, noticing but not paying attention to the looks I was getting from men and women alike, no longer as fascinated as I once was with people's lust for me. All they saw was a pretty piece of pussy, not knowing I could buy or sell any of them like they did so many of my people back in the day.

I took the elevator and found the room without a problem, and not bothering to knock, I strolled in purposefully with my head held high. No guns were drawn and no body-builder types put their hands on me, just three sets of eyes turned their mildly annoyed gaze on me.

Closing the door, I stood before them at the table they occupied and waited, looking at each legend directly before speaking.

"Peace, Almighty."

"Peace to you, Bloodette. Do you know why you've been summoned here?"

"No, sir."

"But you have an idea, huh?"

"I do."

"Then let's not bullshit each other. You know who we are?"

"Sunny Black, Frank White and Iceberg."

"Correct. So then, you understand that you would not be here viewing us in person for anything trivial, right?"

"Yes, sir."

"Good. Have a seat."

I did as I was told and continued to look directly at Sunny Black since it was obvious he was the spokesman for this occasion. My stomach was in knots. It was hard to believe that I was sitting in front of the council. Me! Even though it wasn't a good reason that had me sitting here, it couldn't be completely bad, either. If they wanted me dead, there were easier ways.

"We understand how hard it was to lose your brother. We loved and respected him, too, and on top of that your son was born. How is he, by the way?"

"Billy. Bad. Ass," I replied, smiling.

This earned me what passed for smiles around the table. "More or less. With this understanding we've given you time and space, and loved you through it all, would you agree?"

"I would, and I am eternally grateful."

"And for all the work you've done and the loyalty you displayed, you were rewarded with a top position in this organization, correct?"

"Yes, sir, and I am grateful for that, too."

"So then, why have you neglected your duties so easily and let others eat off our hard work? Have you lost your will for this life? Has your flame gone out?"

"I—"

"Before you answer that," Iceberg said, "I want you to realize who you are talking to and exactly how disrespectful it will be to make bullshit excuses."

I closed my mouth, licked my lips, and started again. "I have no excuse."

The silence was thick as they contemplated my response. I'd put myself at their mercy, which was the smartest thing I could do at that time.

"Are you aware that our operations, all illegal and some legal, have been completely taken over in Virginia and in very important places in Texas?"

I couldn't speak. My tongue was stuck to my mouth and I felt like I'd swallowed a small sheep. How the fuck had I let that happen? Virginia was the biggest state in the half-a-billion-dollar empire I'd helped build for our movement, so I should have protected that at all costs. If I was honest with myself, and now seemed like the perfect time to be, I knew exactly how it had happened. I hadn't set foot in Virginia since.

"I can tell by your expression that you didn't know it was that bad. When was the last time you were down there?"

"I. I. Not since."

"You left everything unattended for five years?"

"I have good soldiers down there."

"You have dead soldiers down there!"

This shit was a lot worse than I thought. Maybe they would kill me. What about my son? I couldn't die, not now. He wouldn't understand, and I needed him to understand. I needed him to know that I loved his father more than anyone I'd ever known, more than anyone I wanted to know. "I fucked up. I have no excuse, and I'll make none. I'm still very much dedicated to our organization and our cause. I'm still Blood, and I'm still Billy until they kill me."

"Let me ask you something. Don't you have a mansion in Virginia?"

"Yeah."

"And do you have any idea who is in your house?"

I did, but could I say it? Did I really have a choice? "My ex-girlfriend. She was pregnant with my brother's baby, so I couldn't just put her out on the streets."

"Who else lives there?"

"I don't know. Why do you ask?"

"Your brother had a wife, right? He just got married?"

"Yeah."

"You get along with her?"

"Yeah, why? What does this have to do with our business?"

"What it has to do with us is we're trying to figure out why these two women are trying to destroy you!"

"Huh?"

"Fuck do you mean, *huh*? You heard me. Let me fill you in. Word is that Ramona Petras is part of the mob, as in Sicilians, and not a small part, either. Her father is Cape Di \ Tutti Capi in Italy, and in the last five years she's made him so happy and so fucking rich that it's pathetic."

"Ramona? Mob?"

"Don't. Make. Me. Repeat. Myself. She's taken over your territory, spilled the blood of our brothers and sisters, and done it all from the comforts of your living room! It's very simple, Keyz:

eat or get ate. We ain't backing down from no noodle-and-pasta-eatin' grease balls. Don't misunderstand, we know how powerful the mob is, but this is our town, our thing, and we run this here, dig me? You have the full support of the EMU Hood behind you, and we're reaching out to let everyone else know the situation. Peace will not be realized without this war. What are you gonna do?"

There was really no need to contemplate. It was time to get back to business, back to the basics. Being Blood was a full-time responsibility. "I'm going to Virginia."

"No. You are going to Virginia tonight."

Aryanna

Chapter Five

Deshana

"Are you gonna answer the phone?" Trey asked.

"Does it look like I'ma answer the phone?"

"Damn, you ain't gotta come at me like that. I was just saying because it's been ringing for the past hour. Forget I said anything, though."

His expression and tone told me that his feelings were hurt, and I kinda felt bad because he didn't deserve it. He was a good guy, a sweet guy, and he already put up with all my bullshit without adding the unnecessary. So why couldn't I just be happy? Did I even know what happiness was anymore? Hell, for all this self-reflection I could go ahead and answer the phone and hear it spoken out loud.

"Look, I'm sorry," I said, sitting on the couch and taking his hand in mine. "I've got a lot on my mind and I'm stressed, but I still shouldn't take that out on you."

"Classes are over for the year, so what's stressing you? Baby, you can talk to me. I hope you know that."

I knew that, but some nightmares didn't deserve a voice. Some things weren't talked about. Ever. It was bad enough simply remembering and living with the constant ache of loss, senseless loss, not to mention the constantly raging hatred that was barely containable beneath the surface of my easy smile and quick tongue. I looked at him, really looked at him, wondering what he'd think of my past and the horrors that still followed me. He wasn't of my world, yet he understood hood politics, struggles, and oppression. But would he understand murder? Cold-blooded murder and everything that came with it? Could he comprehend all that I'd done and all I had to do?

Looking into his hazel eyes, I saw the love he had for me and the concern my silence was creating in him. His love was real, comforting, and pure. But mine? My love died a long time ago, and now all I had to offer were hollow promises and illusions. He deserved more than that, but I had no more to give. I didn't know how.

"It's complicated," I said, reaching for the phone as it started ringing again. "What's crackin'?" I said, smiling at the frustration in her voice.

"Tsk, whatever. I got Sharday on the phone, too."

"I figured that. So, what do I owe the pleasure of this long-distance call?"

"Well, we kinda wanted to talk about the distance part."

"For God's sake, Day-Day, don't beat around the bush!"

"Shut up, La-La!"

"Look, I know you two didn't call me to argue," I said, interrupting the typical sisterly dynamic.

"Deshana, are you coming home or not?" La-La asked impatiently.

I knew this was the reason for their call, I'd known even before I answered the phone. I'd made California my home for the last four years, not once visiting the east coast or the family I'd left on it, but now that school was finished, what was keeping me here? Despite popular belief, it wasn't the six-foot-two, coffee-colored, hazel-eyed nigga next to me, and that should've been a damn good reason. He was everything any normal girl would dream of, but I wasn't normal, and this wasn't a dream.

"We miss you, Lil' M," Day-Day whispered, hurt and need lacing every word.

The truth was I missed them too, more than I'd ever admitted before that moment.

"Dad would want you to come home. He'd want us to be together. And even though I don't say it enough, I miss your ass too, damn it, so come home and annoy the shit out of me already!"

We all laughed even though we knew how true and rare Latavia's words were. La-La wasn't one to wear her heart on her sleeve, she couldn't really afford to. She'd more or less been the backbone of the family since.

"Lil' M?"

"I'm here, Day-Day. I've got a few things to take care of out here, but my flight lands at Dulles around nine o'clock your time."

"Nine o'clock? Tonight? So, bitch, you was already coming home and you made us beg you? Oh, I'ma whoop your ass, Deshana!" La-La yelled, but I could hear the obvious joy in her voice. It brought a smile to my face. I could hear Day-Day's laughter and her sniffling, which meant she was crying. Typical, but I loved her.

"Yeah, I'm coming home, but you can't tell anyone, and I mean it. How's Mom doing?"

The question brought back silence, thick with mixed emotions, none of which outweighed the sadness. "The same, pretty much. She's just going through life on autopilot. I don't know if she'll ever be able to accept his... that he's not here. But they're taking good care of her at St. Elizabeth's."

The tears of joy were replaced with a lump in Day-Day's throat as she made this statement. It was hard on all of us that our mother had slipped into a catatonic state after learning of our father's death, but it had been harder on them because they had to deal with her. I just ran away.

"How's the CD coming along, Day-Day?" I asked, changing the topic to something more pleasant.

"Almost done. It's really good. I think he would've been proud."

"We're all proud of you, and I have no doubt that he is, too. So, do I get an advanced copy, or do I have to wait and pay retail for it?"

"Bring your ass home and I'll sing the motherfucker for you!"

The laughter was back in her voice, and I loved it. I loved her. "I love you both. You know that, right?"

"Of course we know," La-La answered seriously.

"We've always known," Day-Day responded just as seriously.

I'd been gone too long, separated from their love and guidance, but now it was time to go, and to finish what Keyz had started. "Alright, who am I staying with?"

"You can use my penthouse in the city until you decide where you want to live."

"Penthouse, La-La? You got a sugar daddy somewhere, slim?"

"Bitch please, you know ain't no old man could ever keep up with this good shit here!" Our laughter reminded me of the good old days, the simpler times in life. "On the real, though, did you really think I was gonna let that bitch just profit off dad's dedication? He gave her the game, and that shit has a price tag on it, so I got what was ours." La-La was a hell of a lawyer. She was ruthless, determined, and driven: three traits our father had passed on to all of us. "And before you ask, your cut has been in an account in the Caymans since you've been gone. Nobody forgot about you."

"It's not about the money, La-La."

"I know. I know it's about more than that. Are you gonna…?"

"That's not something we need to discuss right now, especially not over the phone. I'll be there soon. Oh, and I'm bringing company with me. So I'm gonna need more room than the penthouse provides."

"No, you won't. We own the building."

"What part of town?"

"Northwest."

All I could do was whistle at that. It was obvious La-La wasn't playing about getting her money's worth out of Keyz's traitorous ass. "Alright, I'll be there soon. Love you both."

They said their *I love you*s and disconnected. Trey had been quiet during my whole conversation, but I could hear him thinking a mile a minute.

Our fingers were still entwined, and I didn't know if his palms were sweating or if it was mine. "Say something."

"What is there to say Deshana? You obviously made up your mind, and one thing I know is that when your mind is made up, that's all there is to it."

"I'm not trying to hurt you, Trey. There are still some things I have to do. Some things you don't know about."

"So tell me about them. Talk to me, baby. I've been begging you to let me in, but knowing the whole time you kept me at arms' length. I still love you. We don't need to have secrets between us."

"Even God has secrets, Trey."

He gently let go of my hand and turned to face me completely. I could see the naked pain in his eyes, and it hurt me, but it wouldn't stop what had to be done.

"For four years you've been a part of my life, first as my friend and now as so much more. For four years you've never talked about your past other than to say where you came from, and not once have you showed any interest in going back. And now all of a sudden you got a fucking flight out like you can't get out of here quick enough. Do I not deserve some kind of answer, or am I supposed to simply accept your decision?"

"Trey Wilson, my decision to leave has nothing to do with you or us."

"Obviously," he said, more than a little hurt.

"But it's not how you think. I've got some unfinished business back home that I put off for long enough."

"So, then when are you coming back?"

I hadn't meant to give him hope. The truth was I didn't know if I'd come back. I didn't know if I'd live through what happened once I let the coldness of revenge take over my heart.

The scary part was that I didn't know if I wanted to.

Needing to put some distance between us, I got up and walked to the balcony, taking a blunt out of the supply I kept rolled and ready by the door and lighting it. The smoke didn't calm my nerves. It wasn't meant to. It focused me, reminded me of the brief times I had with the one man that would forever have my heart and undying devotion.

As I pulled on the blunt, my eyes stared off into the City of Angels, somewhat contemplating where we went, if anywhere, once we died. Where was my dad now?

"You're not coming back, huh?" he said from behind me. The pain in his voice was evident, and if I looked into his eyes, I knew I would see devastation. It wasn't supposed to end like this, not for us. We were supposed to defy the odds, get married and maybe have some kids one day, but most dreams never see the light of reality.

"I don't know, Trey, that's the truth. I'm taking me and my team to finish up some business and, well, shit is gonna get ugly."

"Well then, I'm coming with you."

"No, you've got your own life to live and a bright future to plan."

"And you're not part of that future?"

Still not turning to face him, I sadly shook my head. "I never was," I whispered, willing my vision not to blur with the tears I wanted to shed for hurting this good man. He didn't deserve it, and I didn't deserve him.

"You're right. You're not a part of my future, you are my future. I'm not giving you up, Deshana, but I will let you go. I'll be here when you get back."

I heard him move back into the living room, and then I heard the door close. Only then did I let the tears fall. They weren't just for him or me, but for everything I'd lost in my life, everything that was taken from me. As much as they were tears of sadness, they were also those of determination. It had been five long, hard years since my world came apart, and in that time I waited. Patiently. If I'd learned nothing else from my father, I learned that revenge is the best thing served cold, and I planned to enlighten a lot of people to that fact of life.

Aryanna

Chapter Six

Closing the door as I came back into the living room, I grabbed my keys and cellphone and locked the door to my apartment on the way out. My bags were already in the truck. Getting behind the wheel of my Range Rover, I called my destination and let them know that I was on the way.

I finished my blunt and pulled off into traffic. It wouldn't take me long to get to Long Beach considering traffic wasn't bad, a rare occurrence in LA, but I wasn't complaining. I took in the thick overcast of smog, the smell of food and spices mixed together with exhaust fumes, and the sounds of people, places, and things that barely slept without consciously taking it all in. I was moving on autopilot, already seeing Virginia in my mind in anticipation of what was to come next.

All I saw was blood. Lots of blood. And that was actually the good news. The bad news was that no amount of bloodshed would bring my daddy back, and that thought brought an unbearable hurt that radiated throughout my body. At twenty-three years old, I was definitely a grown woman, but all I wanted was to be a little girl and have my daddy back.

"Get it together, slim. You're coming apart," I said to myself, hoping to feel the familiar numbness that I embraced before unleashing complete chaos.

While I'd come to Cali to go to UCLA, I hadn't exactly changed my ways or reformed. I was still my father's daughter. I was still a killer. Some people kill in self-defense or out of emotional overload, but a real killer did it just because it could be done. It may not necessarily need to be done, but in my book it was the first and best option. My first week here it was the same attitude that got the Rolling 60's Crips' attention and put me in a position of power I now enjoyed.

Driving the familiar streets of east LA, I let my mind roll back to the night that this little black girl became a five-foot-two legend. Thinking about it now, I didn't know what made me get involved in something that wasn't my business, other than the fact that I could get involved. The party in Baldwin Hills was whack, and that's why I stepped outside to smoke a blunt and contemplated the rest of my night. I didn't know what the three bitches were arguing about by the dumpster, or even where the fuck they came from, but they were interrupting my personal time. All that yelling, and for what? It was real simple: if there was an issue, then pluck that bitch's feathers and keep it moving.

They continued to argue, though, and I continued to smoke, somewhat amused because it was obviously two-on-one, but the one was giving it to the two. A little, short, dark-skinned girl about my height only a little healthier was all up in the mugs of the two light-skinned girls towering over her, unafraid and letting them know it. It wasn't until the dark-skinned girl stepped under the streetlights and I noticed the huge *BK* tattooed on her arm that I started paying attention.

The next word I heard was *slob*, and then all hell broke loose. The time for talk was done, and the two girls commenced to whooping ass in a major way. Patches of hair flew, nails popped off, and all ladylike etiquette was forgotten. It was a good, old-school brawl, but it wasn't a fair fight. The two light-skinned girls, obviously Bloods gauging by the red flags tied around their wrists, were dressed almost identical in white wife-beaters, black jeans, and red Chuck Taylors that were presently kicking the shit out of the smaller girl. The only differences I could see so far were the orange and yellow bras and the ponytail versus the close-cut.

None of that mattered, though. All that mattered to me in that moment were those two bird-bitches that represented something I hated. They represented Keyz.

Tossing my blunt, I pulled out my Pearl-handled Baeyer .380 from the back of my jeans and calmly walked up on the girl-fight. I got close enough to the one with the ponytail without her noticing me and watched her body slump as I shot her behind her right ear. Her partner was too focused on stomping the poor dark-skinned girl into the ground to notice what happened, so I tapped her on the shoulder before shooting her twice in the face.

The light brown eyes of the girl with the *BK* tattoo looked at me warily when I extended my hand to her to help her up, but still she took it and I pulled her from the ground. She looked at the two corpses at my feet, spat on them, and pulled me quickly into an alley away from the gathering crowd that was spilling out of the party. I wasn't panicked, and neither was she, but it was understood that I just executed two girls in public and we had to put distance between us and them.

We ran for what seemed like miles until we finally stopped in front of a house in a cul-de-sac.

"Why you shoot them?" "Were they Bloods?"

"Yeah."

"That's why I shot them."

"You a Crip!"

"Nah."

"What gang are you, then?"

"I ain't in one."

"So how did you know they were Bloods?"

"Because I heard you say *slob*."

"And?"

"And what?"

"So you just decided to shoot them because they were Bloods?"

"I shot them for that reason and because I could. You should be careful."

I saw the fire in her eyes come back quick and hot, but she held her tongue. Maybe it was because I still had my gun out. Tucking it in my jeans, I turned to walk away, but she stopped me.

"Thanks."

"It's nothing."

"To me it is. Who are you?"

"Nobody."

"You're far from nobody, but I can understand if you have trust issues. I'm JuJu, Rolling 60's Crip."

"Okay."

"Look, we need to get off the streets for a little while. And this is my spot, so you coming in or what?"

That was a good question, considering I didn't want to go to jail and I was nowhere near my apartment. What did I have to lose?

"A'ight, slim."

"Slim? Oh, you really ain't from around here, huh?"

My answer was the dull look I screwed on my face. I didn't want to think about where I was from or why I wasn't there right now. I didn't want to remember what had sent me 3,000 miles to commit murder as easily as I lit a cigarette. It didn't matter, that was the lie I had to keep telling myself.

Coming back to the present, I pulled up in front of a different house from all those years ago, but it was still the same in the aspect of JuJu standing out front. Looking at her now, it felt like we were two halves of the same whole, my sister-in-arms despite our difference in rank. We had a lot of blood on our hands, and we wanted a lot more. We were driven by life's tragedies. Looking into her light brown eyes from the seat of my truck, I could still see her pain, but I also saw her compassion and the love she had for me. I felt the same. Still five-foot-two, 145 pounds, cute in the face, and thick in the waist, we resembled each other enough to be actual sisters. Our only differences were my blonde locks and almost black eyes versus her boyish cut and light brown eyes. I'd gained my weight in all the right places, allowing my ass to fill out nicely, and that feature alone got us dubbed *The Twins*. It wasn't until we started putting our murder game down seriously that we became *The Casket Twins*.

I turned off the truck and hopped out, hearing the music as soon as my feet hit the pavement and not surprised that it was Snoop bumping from the speakers inside. "What's crackin', cuz?"

"Oh love or no love, cuz."

"Is everybody here?"

"Almost. The guest of honor is."

The guest of honor was none other than Gangsta Boy Blu, official big homey for Harlem Rolling 30's Crips and the nigga I needed to help me with the first phase of my plan. "Well, let's get to it, then. The rest of them niggas and bitches can get caught up on the plane."

We walked into the house, where I was greeted and embraced by about fifty more homies before I was able to take a seat next to Gangsta Boy. The volume of the music was never turned down. They never knew who was listening, and besides, what I had to say had been discussed with those who needed to know. For the most part this was our farewell party. It was understood that all of us wouldn't make it back, but none of us would be dying in vain. That was my promise to them. We were all family, and as I looked around the scarcely furnished living room, I felt the love I held dear for everybody in the living room.

Sitting on the worn brown sofa, I studied the matching thin carpet and gathered my thoughts. I wasn't nervous, I just meant what I said, and so I made sure I only said what I wanted to.

"What's on your mind, twin?" Gangsta Boy asked, lighting a cigarette.

"I'm flying back to the east coast tonight. I've got some unfinished business, and I need your help to finish it."

"I'm listening, cuz."

"A slob killed my Pops five years ago. I want her and everything around her dead."

"You don't need my permission or help to do that. What's the catch?"

"The catch is that the bitch has made her base of operations in New York. It was Virginia, but she hasn't been back since."

"So you want to bring the drama to her front door."

"Yeah."

I could see the wheels turning in his head, weighing exactly what I was asking him to get involved in, but he gave no outward signs of disapproval. I lit a cigarette of my own and waited. Everyone else in the room continued to talk and party, enjoying each other's company and the mood the music created. JuJu's eyes met mine from across the room and I read the question in them, offering a slight shoulder shrug because I didn't have the answer yet.

"What do you need?"

"I need to be plugged on the east and take some homies from out here, too."

"Money?"

"No."

"Weapons?"

"Yes."

"What did your big homie say?"

"I have the complete love and support of the set, if not the whole nation. This has been a long time coming, and I made that known from day one."

"Uh-huh. New York, New York, the city so nice they named it twice. I need two favors from you, Deshana, and I want you to listen before you agree. The first is that there is a traitor among us and he has to be dealt with. Publicly."

"Who?"

"Quick."

This news was like a gut shot. Quick was a big homie. He'd been bangin' for almost forty years! He even claimed to be the illegitimate child of the late Stanley "Tookie" Williams. For him to do something that went against the code seemed impossible, but Gangsta Boy wouldn't say it unless it was true.

"You want to know what he did, huh?"

"That's above my pay grade," I replied, taking a drag off my cigarette and putting it out.

"Actually, it's not. You and JuJu will be OGs after this piece of business is complete. I'm not speaking prematurely. The powers-that-be already discussed and decided how this would go, but only if you wanted. We all feel like you are both ready to take our movement into the next generation, and that brings me to the second thing I need you to do. You go and you do what you have to do, and when the smoke clears, I want there to be a new Queen of New York."

"Who?"

"You."

That statement effectively rendered me speechless. Me take over New York? Seriously? New York was the Blood capital of the East Coast.

All the more reason to take it away from them.

I felt JuJu's eyes on me, and I found her smiling knowingly at me. It was obvious she had some idea what had just been shared, although I doubt she could hear it over Snoop's lyrics.

"Well?"

"It would be my honor."

"Then you have our full support and blessing. And now you have to go."

"Where?"

"Quick is eating lunch right now at Olive Garden with a police lieutenant who's on the take. JuJu is coming with you, and you both can decide how best to handle it. All that matters is that it's done, and done right. Understood?"

"Yeah."

"A'ight then."

And with that, I got up and headed back out front with JuJu right behind me. We stopped out front by my truck.

"Is it on?"

"Are you up for this, Ju?"

"Are you?"

"Without question."

"Then you don't have to question me. I'm by your side until the end."

"Let's ride then."

Once we got moving, JuJu lit a blunt and passed it to me before lighting one for herself. We rode on in a comfortable silence, each looking toward a future that could be long or cut extremely short. One thing was for sure: Quick's number had come up.

"What did he do?"

"He snitched."

"Proven?"

"In black and white."

"Damn. Which Olive Garden?"

"The one out here by the beach."

We continued on, smoking and anticipating what was next to come. Once we got there, we hopped out of the truck and went around the back. I opened it, lifted up the floor compartment, and pulled out our Blood Bag, as we called it. Inside we had wigs, red bandannas, and dirty guns. It was a bit old-fashioned, but we used these props when we needed to bury someone without being suspicious on our own people. All it took was a three-minute change and we became teenage Blood gangbangers.

"JuJu, pull the truck right in front and hit the buttons to change the tags and the paint color. I'll be out in a minute."

A few years back, car companies came up with the technology that allowed a driver to flip the color of his or her car at the press of a button. Not only was it a slick feature, criminals used it to help them get away from crime scenes undetected. Cops would be looking for, say, a blue car, but in a matter of seconds the car's color could be flipped to something else. The feature was very expensive, but worth every dollar.

"Make it rain," said JuJu.

"Blood, that is."

I tucked the two Beretta 9mms inside my hoodie and strolled casually into the restaurant. There wasn't much of a crowd, and that made it easy to spot Quick without being spotted as I made a left and went toward the bathrooms. I didn't spot any cameras, but that didn't mean they weren't there. Of course they were there.

Surprisingly enough, the lieutenant's security was minimal, but then again, he was actually liked by a vast majority of LA. I spotted a three-man team, and of course Quick was all by himself. Who targets an OG in this city? I do.

Making a quick U-turn I headed back into the dining room, flipping off the safeties on the pistols as I went. Before the security could react, I shot two of them in the head and the third one through the heart as he tried to pull his gun out. Quick scrambled for cover, but the lieutenant sat there like he was above death. He discovered how very wrong he was when I put the gun to his head and pulled the trigger mercilessly.

The screams around me were deafening, only adding to the noise factor of breaking glass and upended tables as people fled, praying their lives would be spared. Most would be, but not the motherfucker I had in my sights. When he saw me, recognition was clear, but he never had the chance to utter a word, plea, or apology before I emptied both clips into a face that would never again be mistaken for anything human.

Tucking one gun back into my hoodie, I quickly reloaded the other and threw a red flag on his chest before calmly walking out to a waiting strawberry red Range Rover.

"Nice color," I said, climbing in as she squealed away from the curb.

"Don't worry, I'll change it back to baby blue in a minute."

"It doesn't matter. I'm done with it either way. It's time that we got something more reflective of our status."

"Where to now?"

"Now? Now we go take what's rightfully ours. We take New York."

Chapter Seven

Monica Holford

"Grace?"

"Yes, Ms. Holford?"

"I'm skipping the meeting this morning. Have someone deliver the quarterly reports and I'll review them later."

"Right away, Ms. Holford," she replied dutifully through the intercom.

My mind wasn't focused on meetings, or really on business at all this morning. At least not on this business. I could admit that I'd done damn good for myself, considering the cards I was dealt. Then again, no one ever heard of empires coming easy to anyone.

Staring blindly out the window of my Dallas office at my fleet of trucks, I let my mind wander and retrace its steps to the best of times and the worst of times. A lot of shit was wrong and downright disturbing when growing up in a poverty-stricken environment, but every hood nigga or chick would tell you that good times were still to be had.

Growing up in Virginia I found that those good times made the bad bearable because we needed to smile or risk drowning in our own tears. I refused to drown. Even when I became the too-often statistic of a single black mother, I refused to drown. One of the most valuable lessons I ever learned was that intimate understanding of the relationship between predator and prey, and that kept me from being swallowed up by my environment. Believe it or not, that lesson came with a lot of smiles, because the main one doing the teaching was the love of my life. It may not have been perfect, but few people got to see him and know him like I did. I mean, truthfully speaking, how many dudes really grew up in the heart of the ghetto in Norfolk, Virginia selling drugs, gangbangin', and even putting that murder game down when needed, yet still knew how to love? Just thinking about his high, yellow-ass taking his grandma to church on Easter Sunday made me smile, because while others saw that in contrast to his street persona, I knew that was just Timmy being Timmy. I never expected puppy love to grow into anything epic, but it did, and the planets seemed to align when I had my baby boy.

The thing about life, though, is when it seems perfect and everyone's content, that's when it's turned upside down.

Timmy was my childhood sweetheart: kind, gentle, and loving. But Skino the Don, his alter ego, was ruthless, calculating, and cold blooded. He was a predator, and the streets were his prey. Like so many others before him, he thought he could play the game without paying the cost.

Our love story wasn't the Bonnie and Clyde type because he kept me out of the streets and out of his business. But the streets talk. I knew he was a gangster, I knew he had power I couldn't imagine, and to accumulate that took a savage instinct. Still, he was my Timmy, and that was how I would always think of him. One thing I knew for sure was that there would never be another like him, not for me, this game, or the streets that I'd left behind so long ago. But there would be justice, and not just for him, but for all of us affected by his loss.

I always knew it could eventually come down to Timmy losing his life. I mean, he was entrenched in his Blood gang movement, but hypotheticals never compare to reality's devastating blow.

Some would argue that I'm crazy or I gave up hope because his body has never been found, and nobody was charged with his murder. To that, I'd say they had never been so in love with someone that they didn't know where they ended and the other person began. Most people want that type of love, but when they have it, there could never be a doubt when they lost it. My Timmy was dead. Whether he deserved it or not was a moot point. The facts remained that a son lost his father and a wife lost her husband.

Embracing revenge, I gained a reason to live instead of continuing to exist. Not knowing who to trust or which way to turn, I fled Virginia for the unknowns of Texas, and I began my dedicated study of the streets' darkest secrets. Little Monie became Monica, a mother, a student, a businesswoman, and a gangster.

Growing up, I had very different dreams for my future. Doing hair had been my thing, but in life I had to roll with the punches or get knocked the fuck out. I was far from a square, and I knew I'd learned more by watching Timmy than most had on the block every day of their lives.

The difference between the predator and its prey more often than not came down to one component: patience. Patience allowed for deep analyzing, which allowed the opportunity to not miss a step, because one missed step and that was someone's ass.

For five years I'd been patient, using my husband's legitimate money and connections to make Holford Trucking the leader in transporting both legal and illegal goods around the country. Five years I'd hidden in the shadows, and in some ways in plain sight, knowing eventually my time would come. For five years I'd been invisible because the number one lesson I'd learned was no one can fight what they can't see, not if they expect to win.

I may not have witnessed Timmy's death, but the streets always told the story eventually, and after taking my time to hear the truth and the lies, I finally felt comfortable with what I pieced together. Now it was time to act.

Taking the phone from my pocket, I pressed the number one to connect to the only person who truly mattered to me.

"Hello?"

"Kevin?"

"Hey, Mom. How are you?"

"I'm okay, sweetheart, just a little tired today, but good for an old lady."

"Old, huh? You wouldn't know how to get old. You just keep finding ways to get better," he replied, laughing.

"True. So how are you holding up?"

"I'm cool, Mom. A little anxious, but I'll be fine. Besides, I've got my mother's patience."

"That you do, son, and because of it your reward will be sweeter. Did everything go as you expected it to?"

"For the most part. I played my part to the letter and gave orders for the delivery of information. I'll be leaving shortly so I can get a head start on traffic, then it's off to the meeting in Virginia. Where are you?"

"I'm at the Dallas office right now, going over the transport list and the books, but I'll be home tonight. I've got eyes on the situation in Virginia because it will heat up quick. Remember to stay out of sight until it's time."

"Okay, we'll stay in touch so we can compare notes."

"Okay, baby. I love you, Kev."

"I love you too, Mom," he said before disconnecting the call.

He always made me smile, and I could feel myself doing it now despite the fact that our time had come and the game was on. No matter what, I'd have him in the end, and he'd have me. In between that I expected some deaths, because there were some people who needed killing. If anyone thought the score was even because Devaughn Mitchell was dead, they had the game fucked up.

This wasn't business. This was utterly and completely personal.

Chapter Eight

Ramona

It felt weird to be traveling with so little security after five years of living like the president, weirder still to have lied to Candy. It wasn't that I didn't trust her, because I did, and I definitely loved her as much as I could given the fact that my heart still belonged to my husband. So why lie? I guess for the same reasons that most people did: because the truth had a way of being too fucking complicated! I had no regrets, though, because she wouldn't understand my truth, wouldn't understand what drove me to make the impossible possible and heal the hole in my heart that grew bigger every day I woke up without him by my side.

Just thinking about him caused me pain, but it also brought a genuine smile to my face as I rubbed my stomach and thought about the little miracle floating inside of me. A little girl, my doctor had said, healthy and progressing well for her short 16-week lifespan. It had been an incredibly hard decision to go see the specialist in Akron, Ohio, one I'd had to make on my own because at this point only I knew how my husband would feel and what he would think.

I had money, power, and fear where there wasn't respect, but none of these things compared to the beautiful little girl I was going to bring into the world in approximately seven months. None of it mattered without her. A miracle.

It seemed like I'd already picked out her name, because I couldn't think of her in any other way except a miracle. Now there'd be two Lil' Ms in the family.

Thoughts of Deshana brought me back to the bustling city around me. It's not like I expected to see her on the streets of New York, but I wondered how she was doing out in Cali. So many times I'd wanted to call her, to go to her, but I understood her need for time when it came to the loss we all suffered.

I couldn't deny that I had selfish motivations as well, but who doesn't in life? It'd been too long, though, and the longer everyone went without closure the worse life would be.

First things first, Keyz had to die, and it was my hope that my very resourceful father had found a way to do it. I could think of no other reason for him to leave the beautiful countryside of Palermo and come to New York, let alone summon me here when he knew this was Keyz's new base of operations. Everything else of the bitch's belonged to me.

Looking out the window, I caught myself smiling until I saw a glimpse of something that turned my blood cold.

"Stop the car!"

"Ms. Mitchell?"

"Stop the goddamn car!" I screamed, already opening the door with my gun out, training it on a black BMW that had just leapt into traffic.

Just as I was preparing to squeeze off round after round, the sounds of impatient horns honking reached my conscious mind, alerting me to the fact I was about to engage in a gun battle in broad daylight on the streets of New York. I didn't need to visit the inside of Riker's Island, and truthfully I couldn't be sure if I actually saw the bitch or if I conjured her in my mind because I wanted her blood on my hands that bad.

"Ms. Mitchell, we need to go," my driver said, pushing my gun back out of sight as he helped me back into the car. There was no need to argue or fight. I'd caused enough of a scene.

Taking a deep breath, I laid the Glock .40 on the seat next to me and reached for a blunt from the ready supply kept in my purse. I was beyond stressed, and that couldn't be good for the baby, but my doctor said occasional weed smoke wouldn't cause any birth defects or bring problems for my little girl.

From the first pull, I felt a release, like I'd been underwater for minutes holding my breath. Closing my eyes, I let the haze envelop me and hold me like my lover used to, wishing that I could go back and feel the real thing if only for a moment.

Too soon I felt the Burgundy 700 Benz glide to a stop and the breeze toss my curls as the driver held the door open for me. Putting out the blunt, I put the pistol back in my purse and threw on my Dolce & Gabbana sunglasses before exiting the car. Head up, eyes alert, I scanned everything and everyone in my immediate vicinity even though I knew it was safe because I was back home.

For my first eight years of life, I ran the streets of Hell's Kitchen, afraid of nothing and no one because even though I didn't know why, I knew my Pop was a big deal. He was more than a man, he was my hero.

"Papa!" I squealed, all the little girl coming out in me as I strolled into Junior's Pizzeria and saw my old man sitting in his favorite booth. His smile was like gold, going all the way up to his onyx-colored eyes that matched my own and showing the prominent laugh lines that enriched the handsome man he was.

"My beautiful Mona," he said in his heavy accent, opening his arms wide and allowing me into the one place I could call home above all else. We exchanged kisses, and then I took my seat opposite him, even though I wanted to stay in his lap forever.

"How are you, Papa?"

"Ah, you know your old man. I could complain, but life is too good to lie."

"I'm glad," I replied, laughing as I removed my glasses and took his hand in my own. Life hadn't always been so good or so easy for him, especially coming from the old country, but he'd made a way, and then made a way for me. He was a hard-working man, and I admired that. Devaughn's ambition reminded me a lot of him.

"Hey, why the frown? You're not happy to see me?"

"Of course, Papa. I just have a lot on my mind."

"I can understand that. And I've come to help."

Deep down, I knew this was the reason he'd come to the states, but I didn't want him on the front line. I couldn't stand the thought of anything happening to him too.

"Help?"

"Yes, help. Do you not think I'm able to help you any longer?"

"I know better than that, Papa. I just don't want you in the line of fire. This is my war."

"It's your war, not my war? You are my only child, and although I will forever love your mother, God rest her soul, I will not have you going to join her at such an early age."

I could see his love for me as clear as day in his eyes, just as well as I could see the steel determination that had driven him for so many years. He meant to have his way, and there was no way around that. "You're right, Papa."

"Of course I am," he said, smiling and signaling the waiter to bring us some food out. I never had to order when I was with him. He was very old school that way, plus he knew all the things I liked to eat. Well, almost all the things I liked to eat.

I smiled to myself, thinking about Candy and on our time together this morning, wishing I was still at home, in between her thick thighs, sucking on her pretty pussy. I never used to have a thing for females. Candy was my first, and undoubtedly she'd be my last.

My love for her was in two parts. I loved her for her, because she was loyal, honest, and sincere. I also loved her because he did, and it made me feel close to him to be with her. Somehow I think he would have wanted it this way, would have wanted us to come together and build a bond that was indestructible, and I loved that his son could witness us coming together from our worlds being shattered. We'd never be the same without him, but every day we'd try to be better than the day before.

"Hope you're hungry," the waiter said, setting a large sausage and pepperoni pizza in front of me, causing my mouth to water and my nostrils to flare.

"Oh, I think she'll manage," my dad said with a laugh as he dug into his tortellini.

For the next two hours we ate and laughed. We reminisced about old times, enjoying each other's company without the complications of the demons lurking in the shadows. I'd always been my daddy's girl, and it felt good to simply be that again for a while. Secretly, I think we both wished it could go back to the way it was once upon a time, but after experiencing the love of my husband, I knew in my heart that I could have no regrets.

"So, Dad, how were you thinking about helping me?" I asked, pushing my empty pizza pan away and lighting a much-needed cigarette.

"Well, first things first, I have some exciting news I want to deliver in person. Over the last five years you made tremendous moves in the underworld, earned a respected name for yourself, and made a lot of money without the assistance or handholding of me and my constituents. I know your intent was one of revenge, but all you have done cannot be overlooked, because you have proven yourself adept at this way of life."

"I'm my father's daughter," I said, smiling.

"Ah, ma tu sei tanto più, mio amore." *But you are so much more, my love.* I loved hearing my father speak Italian. "You are the future! And that's why you're being made."

It seemed like something suddenly went wrong with my hearing, because everything he said made sense up until that last part. "Made?"

"Yes, made."

"As in?"

"As in you're being an official member of this thing of ours. Forever entrenched in its history, and sworn to uphold its laws above all else."

"But I'm a girl."

This comment brought me laughter rich with good humor and love. "I'm aware you are a woman, sweetheart."

"But. But the rules."

"The rules have been revised."

"But I'm not full-blooded Sicilian."

"Trust me, you're more Sicilian than most of them."

"But." I could think of nothing else to say. I was being made, and this wasn't no TV shit. I was actually about to embark on a journey that would forever change the rest of my life, and the lives of little Italian girls everywhere. Including my own little girl. "Pop, I gotta tell you something before I can accept this honor. I'm pregnant."

I could tell by the look of utter confusion on his face that I had some serious explaining to do, so before I lost my nerve, I poured out all the details on how I had used invitro to get pregnant. Not a conversation a girl wants to have with her father, but the circumstances dictated that it was necessary.

I was greeted with a thick silence once I was done talking, and I knew he had to be the one to break it, but I was apprehensive about what he might say. I knew he'd accept my decision regardless. I just didn't want to disappoint him.

"Who knows about it?"

"No one."

"A miracle."

"My sentiments exactly. So now you understand why it's not possible for me to accept this great honor?"

"No, I don't see that. We are not a gang, sweetheart. We are a family, and family will always stick together. At least this family will. You being pregnant changes nothing, so if you're refusing, I'm gonna need a better reason than that."

A better reason? Shit, I thought I'd pretty much hit a home run with that one right there! Realizing I needed something way stronger than a cigarette, I fished in my purse until I found my blunt case, at which point I had to silence my father with a warning look as I fired up and inhaled the potent smoke. A made woman? Me? Wow! What would Candy say? What would Devaughn say? He'd probably give me that lazy smile of his and say something like, "Aw, shit, now I'm really not fucking with you."

With a smile on my face, I gazed lovingly into my father's eyes and nodded my ascent, then I leaned forward and kissed his ring. "I love you, Papa."

"And I love you too, my baby. Now, we have much to do for your ceremony tonight."

"Tonight?"

"Yes, tonight. You know I must return home at the earliest possible opportunity. I no longer have a desire to be here in the states. But before we get to that, we have another piece of business that we must attend to."

"Do we?"

"Yes. Come," he said, taking my hand and leading me from the table toward the stairs leading to the basement.

Aryanna

Chapter Nine

I'd never been in the basement of Junior's before. It was expressly forbidden, but I guess I had carte blanche now that I was to be an official member of La Costra Nostra.

As we came to the bottom of the stairs, we encountered a steel door. There was no special knock or any such nonsense seen in old movies. The door slid soundlessly open and we continued on down a darkened corridor until we came to an identical door. This one required a palm print for entry, and my father told me to put my hand on the scanner, which to my surprise opened it immediately. Leave it to my old man to waste no time in making sure I had access to all parts of his world, although now it was our world.

When I first entered the room, I noticed how cold it was in there. Damn near at freezing level, which was in complete contrast to the heat of summer upstairs. My eyes took in the cold, dark room, locking in on what appeared to be a woman huddled in the far corner. I could tell she was alive because I could hear her teeth chattering from over here, but her back was to me, so I couldn't see her. She was the right height, right build. Could it be? "Is that?"

"I wish it were, sweetheart, but it's someone close enough to deliver a message."

At the sound of our voices, she spun around, revealing two things. One was her face, which I imagined was quite beautiful at one point, but now resembled a horrible accident victim with all the swelling, cuts, and bruising. The second thing she revealed was that she wasn't alone, but one look at her companion told me all I needed to know, because even from this distance I knew that face.

My legs moved of their own accord, bringing me closer to the couple until I was standing right over top of them, my attention focused solely on him. "What's your name?" I asked, just above a whisper.

He didn't say anything, but it wasn't fear I saw in his eyes. He was evaluating me just as calmly as if we were sharing a meal together instead of in a freezer that had probably been the last site for many a man.

"Your name?" I asked again, taking a step closer to him.

"Don't say anything," the woman mumbled through swollen lips, but I could still see that he'd make his own decisions based on whatever conclusions he came to.

"You interrupted my basketball game," he said finally, allowing more than slight agitation to flood his dark brown eyes.

"Did I? Who was playing?"

"The Knicks and Boston, but Boston doesn't stand a chance."

I smiled at him, liking him instantly, but I could tell he would not be won over by something as simple as my smile.

"Why did those men hurt my aunt?"

"She your aunt?"

"Yeah."

"So who's your mom?"

This question wasn't answered, but I didn't need it because I knew who his father was. "What's your name?" I asked for the third time, trying not to let my impatience show.

"Leave him alone," the woman said, pushing him behind her as she stood up. The look in my eyes should have been warning enough, but it was evident she loved the little boy and would protect him with her life, should it come to that.

"Okay, then what's your name?"

"Ask your goons who beat me up. They have all my info."

"Dad?"

"Her name is Victoria Williams, 30 years old, and she's the girlfriend of one Kiara Briggs, better known as Keyz. The little boy is Devonte Mitchell, Keyz's son. And your stepson."

Somehow even when someone knows the truth, it still has a way of sucker punching and knocking all the wind out of a person. It was plain to see this was Devaughn's little boy. He looked just like his father and his brother D.J.

"Look, do whatever you have to do to me, but let him go. He's just a kid, for Christ's sake!"

Just a kid? Nah, he wasn't just a kid. He was Devaughn's kid. He was Keyz's kid. And he was my own kids' big brother. How he ended up in this situation was so beyond my comprehension, but one thing I knew for sure was that I couldn't kill him. I hated his mother, and I knew his death would bring her to her knees, but I also knew killing my husband's son was something he could never forgive me for.

Still, a message had to be sent. "Dad, I need a blanket, a permanent marker, and a scalpel. And strap this bitch to a chair, too. I don't want her trying to run anywhere or put up a fight. Victoria, for your cooperation, I promise not to harm a single hair on Devonte's head, but if you make it hard, I'll make it harder."

She stared me down in a test of wills, but she knew as well as I that she was in a no-win situation. Her number was up, plain and simple. The only question that remained was would she be a gangsta about this shit?

She mouthed the word *okay* as she turned and squatted in front of the little figure behind her. "Tay, you know I love you, right?"

"Yeah."

"And you know I love your mommy, right?"

"Yeah."

"Well, I need you to do me a favor and make sure you tell her how much I love her, okay?"

"Why can't you tell her?"

"Because, baby. Because I'm not going with you when you leave here."

I saw how he just looked at her for a minute, and then his eyes locked onto mine with an almost startling clarity. He definitely possessed his father's intellect and ability to assess situations.

"Okay, Aunt Vita, I'll do that for you," he said, hugging her tightly. His big, brown eyes filling with tears that pricked my conscience a little. Only a little, though.

"Here," my father said, handing me the things I asked for and resuming his position by the now-closed door.

"In the chair, Victoria," I directed, taking the blanket over to Devonte and wrapping it around his shaking shoulders.

"You need to take him somewhere else so he doesn't have to see this," I heard her say as she was being strapped down to the metal chair. I agreed with her because I didn't want him to see what was about to happen, but he needed to see it so she could see it through his eyes.

"Don't move from this spot," I told him, sitting him up against the far wall.

"Get him outta here!" she screamed, wrestling futility with her restraints.

Without a word, I picked up the scalpel, moving to stand directly behind her chair, and grabbed a fistful of her hair to keep her from squirming.

"Not like this. Please, not like this. Not in front of him!"

He was looking at me, and I could feel the power of his stare even as wave after wave of tears cascaded down his young face.

"Look away, Tay!" she screamed when I yanked her head back, exposing her beautiful, caramel-complexion neck, but still his gaze remained fastened on me, on my eyes, almost like he was challenging me.

Slowly, I dragged the scalpel across her throat, cutting her voice off mid-scream and leaving only the sounds of her gurgling on her own blood to occupy the silence of the room. Her life drained out of her in a warm rush over my delicate fingers, giving me a small feeling of vindication that I knew would explode to orgasmic proportions once it was Keyz's blood flowing freely through my fingers.

Letting her head drop, I slowly walked to the little boy who was still staring at me with a quiet rage, blinded by his own tears, but defiant and wiping them away. "Turn around," I told him, exchanging the scalpel for the permanent marker.

Wordlessly, he did as I commanded. He didn't fight me when I removed the blanket so I could lift up his jersey. Quickly I scribbled my message on his back, then turned him around to face me.

"When you get home, I want you to tell your mother what you saw here today, then I want you to take off your jersey and show her your back."

Silence was still his response to all I'd said, but I didn't really expect him to say anything because he was probably in shock. "You may hate me for doing what I did to your aunt, and that's okay, but consider yourself lucky because it could've been you. The only reason it wasn't you is because I love your daddy very much."

"You-you know my daddy?"

"Once upon a time, he was my whole world," I replied with tears clouding my own vision.

"You're not a nice lady. But will you tell me who my dad is?"

"You don't know?" I asked, somewhat astonished. He just shook his small little head, and at that moment I actually felt bad because he'd been cheated in so many more ways than I could've imagined. I turned and looked at my own father, my rock in any storm, and I saw the love that he'd always have for me no matter what I did, and I realized that this little boy might not know that.

"How much time before the ceremony, Pop?"

"You have time."

"Come on," I said, taking his tiny hand in my own and leading him out of the basement. He'd never be the same after today, but that didn't have to be a completely bad thing.

.

Chapter Ten

Candy

Pop! Pop, pop, pop, pop, pop! Pop, pop!

I couldn't hear my son's applause, but I could see his enthusiastic little hands coming together as I put bullet after bullet in the targets I had put up in the backyard. This had become a ritual for us: first I'd take him to spend time with Devaughn, and then we'd come out here so I could try to bleed some of the hate and loneliness out of my system. I felt so much of these emotions that at times I was surprised I hadn't been consumed by them yet, but then DJ would smile, and my heart would swell with the knowledge that God had given me this little savior to keep me going in these very trying times. Some days it felt like I was living the book of Job, but I knew it could be worse. A lot worse.

Releasing the clip from the .45, I quickly slid another one into place and sighted the target farther away from me, regulating my breathing until I felt my whole body relax and float through my fingertips into this precious and lethal steel I cradled lovingly. Closing my eyes, I let my mind see the target as it had been, squeezing off round after round until the sharp click of the empty chamber reverberated through my hands.

Where once stood a life-size mannequin posting a picture of Keyz, now only dust remained, proving my new exploding Black Talon rounds worked perfectly at a substantial range. Excellent, but truthfully I didn't want to kill the bitch from a distance. I wanted to stand over her and looked deep into her eyes before I sent her straight past hell.

I looked down, feeling DJ pulling on my shorts, and followed his hand motions to the maid coming toward me with a phone in her hand. "Go wash up for lunch," I told him, pulling off my protective headphones and taking the phone offered me. "Yeah?"

"Candy?"

"Yeah, who is this?"

"It's me."

"Me? Deshana, is that you?"

"Yeah. I know, you're surprised, huh?"

"Um, hell yeah, but it's a great surprise. How are you? How have you been?" I asked, walking to the patio and sitting down.

"I've been okay, mostly busy with school and shit."

"And shit?"

"Yeah, you know me, Candy. I'm my father's daughter."

"Yeah, I know," I whispered, my heart hurting at the memory of just how much they loved each other. There was a bond that not even death can separate, a loss that not even time can heal. The fact was that for the last five years, time had stood still for everybody, and there was no doubt in my mind that it had been the same way for her. "So how's school?"

"It's done. I graduated with a BA in business, Dean's list and all."

"Congratulations! I know he'd be extremely proud of you. So what's next?"

"You know what's next. I can't do anything until this is resolved completely."

"I-I understand that. We feel the same way."

"We?"

"Ramona and I. After your father, we just…. It's complicated."

"Far be it for me to judge. If you make each other happy, I think that's what you'd want above all else."

"There is no happiness without him, but we managed to make it from one day to the next. It's still hard."

"And your baby?"

"DJ is fine. He's so much like his daddy that it'll make your heart hurt, but overall he's a happy child."

"DJ, huh?"

"Yeah, I figured your dad would have wanted a Junior. It fits him."

"Yeah, he would've. I'm sorry I haven't been there for you or him."

"We don't blame you, Lil' M. We all had to deal with what happened the best way we could. We all loved him differently, yet completely, so everyone had to try dealing in their own way."

"Are you healed?" she whispered, emotion choking her so fiercely that I could hear her tears she wouldn't shed.

"Never. I'll never heal."

For a while we just let the silence speak for us, both of us trapped inside a hell that offered no escape. One man and the love we all had for him had altered our lives to the point that a future without him was unrecognizable, and therefore unwanted. But none of us would stop until that bitch was in the ground where she belonged.

"So what are your plans?"

"Plans? I've got a lot of plans, but I need you and Ramona's help."

"Anything."

"My flight is coming in early, so."

"Wait a minute, your flight? You're coming home?"

"Yeah, and we'll be landing in about two hours."

"We?"

"I brought a few friends along with me, but don't worry, we'll be staying at La-La's penthouse in the city."

"There's room here, you know that."

"Actually, I was thinking I might stay there. That way I could spend some time with DJ, if that's okay with you."

"Of course it is. You can stay in the main house or the little house with Jordyn."

"Jordyn still lives there?"

"Yeah, your other sisters didn't tell you?"

"I never asked. After the shit with her father, I couldn't face her."

I didn't know what to say to that. I'd been in the room when she tortured Craig with a razor blade and some scalding black oil before she executed him. She showed him no mercy, but when a man deserves to die, his killer is rarely merciful.

"I'll set up a room close to DJ's. What else do you need?"

"Can you send someone to scoop us up from the airport?"

"No problem. How deep is your crew?"

"We ten strong on this flight. Everybody else will arrive later."

"What airport?"

"Dulles International."

"Why didn't you just call sooner? You know we woulda sent one of the jets to get you?"

"One of the jets? What, did y'all hit the lottery or something?"

"Or something. Everything that belonged to Keyz in Virginia and parts of Texas now belongs to Mona and me."

Her whistle was long and deep. "You all have been busy," she said, laughing.

"Of course. Whatever you want is yours, Deshana. We know how much he loved you, and he would've given you the world on a silver platter."

"I know. Thank you for that."

"You ain't gotta thank me, just get your ass out here, bitch!" I said, laughing to lighten up the mood.

"Bitch, I'm on the way. Driving ain't like flying, and since I don't know how to fly, I'ma let the pilot do the damn thing. Will you have somebody meet us, though?"

"You never have to ask twice. When you get off the airplane, stay on the tarmac, because I'm sending two helicopters to get you. Call La-La and let her know what's good so your people can get settled, and then all three of you fly out here for dinner tonight. It's going to be a family affair. The prodigal daughter has returned home!"

I could hear her laughing with a richness reminiscent of her father. It was crazy how all his kids had some variation of that laugh, but it was sweet music to my ears. "Alright. I'll be there in a minute, and I'm bringing my home girl with me, too."

"Oh, you playing for my team now, too?"

"Bitch, hell nah!" she replied, laughing again.

"Ain't nothing wrong with it. Don't knock it until you tried it, slim."

"I'll take your word for it, and I'll see your crazy ass soon."

"Cool."

"Hey, Candy?"

"Yeah?"

"Thanks."

"You know I gotchu, Lil' M," I replied, disconnecting our call and sitting back to contemplate all that her arrival meant.

She was only coming back for one reason, and she was just as determined as we were to see that bitch dead, so I welcomed her with open arms. But I couldn't allow anything to happen to her. Only a few years separated us in age, despite the fact that the tragedy we'd suffered had aged us more. But still I had to look after her, because it's what he would want.

"Who was on the phone, Mommy? Was it Mona?" DJ asked, coming around the corner with a PB & J sandwich in his hands.

Ordinarily I'd make him eat it in the kitchen, but I didn't feel like having that particular fight today.

"That was your sister, baby."

"Which one?" he asked with that *Duh, Mom, I have more than one* look that was so cute I couldn't even get mad at him for it.

"Your sister Deshana."

"The one I haven't met?"

"Yep, that one."

"Oh. How is she?"

"She is good, and actually she'll be here in a few hours for dinner."

"Cool!"

"Very cool indeed. So, what should we have for dinner?"

"Um, fried chicken. And macaroni and cheese. And mashed potatoes. And cookies. And…."

"Hold up, you're forgetting a vegetable."

"Aw, Mom!"

"Aw, Mom nothing. Either you pick or I will."

I could see his little brain working overtime trying to figure out a way around or under the vegetable rule, and I admired his effort, but he knew there was no way around it. "Carrots," he said sullenly, causing me to laugh as I pulled him in close for a hug.

I was glad he was still at that age where it was okay for me to hug him, because Lord knows I was dreading the day when that changed. "Do you want to Skype with me when I let Mona know the good news?"

"Yeah, and then can I go to Daddy?"

"Sure you can, baby. Go get my laptop and bring it back over here."

He scurried off at the lightning pace mastered by all toddlers, giving me a much-needed moment to catch my breath as I thought about the way he talked to a man who would never answer him. I prayed he could simply hear him and knew that his son loved him beyond explanation or reason. It hurt me beyond words, but I knew I was doing the right thing in keeping Devaughn a part of DJ's everyday life. My son would know, love, and respect his father, dead or alive. I barely remembered my own father, so at the very least I owed DJ this.

I flipped the safety on the .45 and tucked it in the waist of my jean shorts when I saw the door open and my little man come out, balancing my laptop precariously. He could break it a million times over and I'd still replace it, but I wanted to instill responsibility into him early on because it builds character.

"Here you go, Mom," he said, standing next to me as I pulled the table in front of us and set up shop to Skype 30,000 feet above the ocean. It wasn't likely she was in Palermo yet.

"Hey babe," I said when her face popped up on her handheld.

"Hey yourself, beautiful. What are you up to?"

"Nothing much. I."

"Hi, Mona!" DJ yelled, waving his hands enthusiastically.

"Hey, little man, what's up?"

"Shit. I mean, nothing," he replied, ducking like a pro when I went to slap him upside his head. Smartass. "Guess what?"

"What?"

"My sister is coming to dinner."

"Oh yeah? Which one?"

"De-De-Deshana, right, Mom?" he asked, looking at me to make sure he pronounced it right.

"You can say *shit*, but you have trouble pronouncing your sister's name?"

"Shit is easier," he said, laughing when I swung again and missed. Smartass.

"Deshana's back?" Ramona asked, her attention now intently on me.

"She will be in a few hours. She's come to finish things up."

"I bet. Does she know?"

"Of course not. Did you think I just blurted that out? We still got two years, and we've been cautious, so why fuck up now?"

"Just asking, no need to bite my head off."

"Sorry. Just a little tense."

"Really? Well, maybe I can help you out with that," she said, smiling seductively.

Damn if my pussy didn't get wet just from her smile! "Behave," I told her, nodding toward my very observant five-year-old who was going on twenty-five.

"So what did Lil' M say?"

"Just that she's finished school and now she's back to finish up that other business."

"Hmm. Where is she staying?"

"With us. I didn't see it as a problem."

"Never would be, but does she know about us?"

"Yeah, I told her, and I think she understands. Or maybe she just doesn't care. She's focused."

"I would imagine so. That's not a bad thing, though."

"No, and it's time for this shit to end. It's been too long."

"Mom, you said shit," my son pointed out with a smile, but that smile quickly faded when I popped him upside his head.

"You lucky I don't pop you twice for ducking, but don't start acting like it's okay for you to cuss, because you're not grown. Hear me?"

"Yes, ma'am," he replied sullenly, giving me a hug with hopes of being sweet and getting back in my good graces. I never could stay mad at him anyway.

"So what time is dinner?"

"About 8:00 p.m., but I can reschedule it if you want to come."

"No, it's okay."

"So the menu is chicken and…. Hold up, Mona, where are you?"

"Huh?"

"Nah, bitch, I ain't say huh. I said where the fuck are you, because I swear that sign behind you says Junior's." Her eyes were as good as saying yes, and her body language reeked of one thing: guilt. "You lied to me?"

"Baby, listen."

"You-you actually lied to me?"

"Candy, I can explain, and I promise it's nothing like what you're thinking."

"How the fuck do you know what I'm thinking?"

"I don't know, but I know it ain't good. I'll be home in a couple hours, and I can explain it all then."

"Fuck all that, slim, explain it to me now. Break it down for a bitch that is obviously slow. Are you at Junior's?"

"Yes."

"Is this the Junior's that is in New York? In Hell's Kitchen to be more exact?"

"Yes, but."

"But ass, bitch, you lied plain and simple! You're supposed to be with your father right now."

"I am with my father."

"Where he at?"

With this question, her handheld swiveled quickly until her father came into view with a sheepish look on his face before she turned it back toward herself.

"So why don't you just say you were going to New York? Whole time had me worried that you were going all the way to Italy."

"It's complicated."

"I suggest you uncomplicated with some quickness or be ready to box once you get back!"

"Can we talk about this when I get home?"

"Nah, we could've talked about it when you were home, but you wanted to be all sneaky and shit. Talk now or sleep in Italy tonight."

I could see her weighing her options and at the same time mentally kicking herself. Whether it was for lying or getting caught, I didn't know, but what I did know was that I didn't appreciate either, because that's not how we rocked. "Well?" I asked, crossing my arms over my chest in my best no-nonsense pose. I could see the defeat in the slump of her shoulders, but she uttered not a word. Instead, she turned her handheld until a face popped up on the screen that stole my breath and vice-gripped my heart. It couldn't be!

"Mom? Mama, who's that boy?"

Chapter Eleven

Kevin Holford

"There's a call for you, sir."

"Thank you. Bring me another shot of Hennessy, please," I told her, admiring her juicy ass as she struggled to maintain her balance with all the air turbulence. It didn't matter how much money someone spent on an airplane, once it was in the sky it was subject to the elements and their moods. It was the one thing I hated about flying, but watching her big ass shake as she walked away from me made today's fight worth it for sure.

"I'm listening," I said into the phone, reclining my seat and getting a little more comfortable.

"It's done."

"Details."

"Keyz's superiors were notified of exactly how out of pocket she's let shit get in Virginia, and they've ordered her to return to active duty immediately. Mr. Petras was provided information and opportunity to go after those close to Keyz, and we both know that his daughter won't pass that up. I've done what you asked, now give me my family back," he growled.

I could feel his anger and desperation coming through the invisible link in our call. I knew how helpless he felt and how badly that crippled a man whose position was used to wielding his power. Knowing all this made me smile. "Patience, Mr. Vick. Remember, you are in no position to make demands considering it was you who betrayed my father for some chump change. And I suggest you remember who the fuck you are talking to before you start receiving body parts in the mail! Now, you'll get your family when mine is satisfied, and right now we're not. Wait for my call," I ordered, hanging up and handing the phone back to the stewardess in exchange for my drink.

"Anything else, Mr. Holford?" she asked, paying close attention to my hand that was slowly unzipping my pants. I said nothing, just whipped my dick out and took a sip of the dark amber liquid I was holding. The hunger in her eyes matched the purring in her throat as she stretched out on the plush leather couch in front of my seat. I felt the softness of her lips and the heat of her mouth as she took as much of me as she could, already pushing my mind far away from there.

She was good, very good, but the satisfaction I felt building inside me came from all of my hard work and plans coming together. For years me and my mother had suffered in silence and endured the pain of our loss while keeping a front firmly in place. But the days of fronting were at their end, and now it was time to make some people answer for what they'd done. Now it was finally time to allow my father peace wherever he rested, as well as give him company, which could extract its own form of justice. And the best part about it was that no one saw us coming! No one remembered that real blood was thicker than water. They would learn, though. Every. Last. One of them would learn.

The dual satisfaction of watching my plans come together along with watching a beautiful, thick, chocolate goddess devour my dick with the suction power of a vacuum made my climax almost instantaneous. She didn't miss a single drop as I exploded in her mouth so hard my body trembled, and I could feel beads of perspiration forming a river down my face.

"Mm," she murmured, swallowing visibly and putting my dick away before getting up and making her way back to the front of the plane. I wanted more, but I was appreciative of the fact that she knew I had business to handle.

Still sipping my drink, I dialed another number and listened to the phone ring a few thousand miles away.

"Heart Foundation."

"Yeah, this is Holford for Murdaheart."

"Hold on."

I didn't know why I expected elevator music every time I made this call. Heart Foundation sounded official, but it was just another name for the Valentine Blood headquarters, and at the end of the day they were nothing more than common gangbangers. That probably seemed hypocritical considering that my old man led EMU on the east coast, but he turned bangin' into an art form. He had come from the streets and transformed himself into a businessman because he understood how the world worked.

Then there were muthafuckas like Devaughn Mitchell who thought the world owed them something, like he was entitled to it all! He was a coward! And in the end he had left his family to atone for his mistakes. They'd pay in blood.

"Sup, Kev?" he said, snapping my focus back onto what needed to be done now.

"Everything is moving smooth. Take care of the Vicks and your money will be deposited before I land."

"Before you land? Where are you going?"

"I'm coming to get a front row seat, of course."

"Isn't that risky? I mean, you'd be spotted immediately."

"Nah, I won't, because hell has no fury like a woman scorned. I'm not the focus. I'm not even a ghost to them, because I never existed."

"True. I will handle the business, just handle yours."

There was no need for me to respond, so I simply hung up. Even though the Bloods had betrayed my father, aligning myself with Murdaheart had still been a necessary evil. If loyalties were to the almighty dollar, then when this was all over he would also see why money was the root of all evil.

The colder the revenge, the better. And my plan was sub zero.

Chapter Twelve

Keyz

I couldn't hear the constant New York noise around me. I couldn't see the millions of people going about their everyday model-American lives. All I could see and sense was home, how close I'd come to making my son, my only reason for living, an orphan. How in the fuck had I been so careless? The truth was I hadn't been careless. I'd been afraid. Afraid of Candy and Ramona, and most of all what I'd done to the only man I'd ever truly loved in my lifetime. But fear was a powerful tool, and now I had to let the fear of certain death motivate me to take back what was mine. I had to tap into the same ruthless bloodlust that had made me a tyrant before I was twenty-five years old, and I had to do it quickly.

Pulling my phone from my purse as I slid into the back of my BMW, I dialed a number I hadn't had cause to use in quite a while.

"Where to, Ms. Keyz?"

"Home. I have some packing to do before we take a quick trip out of town. Text my head of security and let him know that I need to meet with him directly after the basketball game."

"I'm on it," the driver said, speeding off into traffic.

The phone continued to ring in my ear until it was finally answered by a breathless, yet familiar voice.

"It's me."

"Uh-huh."

"I am coming down there."

"When?"

"In a few hours."

"Isn't that a coincidence, considering Deshana is returning to the east coast, too," she replied, sarcasm and anger lacing her words.

"When?"

"She'll be back tonight. There's some type of dinner at your old house."

"And who will be there?"

"Everybody, for the most part."

"Make sure you save me a seat."

"So it's time, then?"

"It is. Are you sure you're ready for this? Because we ain't talking hypothetical no more. It's kill or be killed."

A heavy silence greeted my question, but I could feel her rage in the air, traveling through the phone and touching me as if we were sharing the same space. I knew nothing would stop her, just as I understood that nothing would stop those motivated to see my own demise. Only I could stop them.

"I'm ready. What do you need me to do?"

"I know the layout, but I need intel, and I need you to shut off the motion sensor lights in the back of the house."

"How?"

"The fuse box is in the…. In the room one floor below the main."

"What room?"

"You know exactly what room I'm talking about. Can you do it?"

"And what else?"

"When the lights go out, have your target in your sites, because shit is gonna get real ugly real quick."

"I'll be ready," she replied, disconnecting.

I wasn't supremely confident in her warrior abilities, but she was my safest bet to get inside. I wanted this over with so I could go back to the important things in life. My priorities had definitely changed, but there was no permanent plan for gang members. Once they're in, they're in, and death was the cost of going out. There was a time in my life when that had made sense because that's what he believed, and I had believed in him if nothing else.

God, I still loved that man! What I'd give to simply have those last moments back, but there were no do-overs in life. The cards didn't get reshuffled. Everyone just played what they were dealt.

As the car glided to a stop, I pulled a blunt from my purse and lit it on my walk to the elevator, even though I knew it'd take a lot more than this to relax me at this point. It seemed like years ago instead of hours when I'd got my nut off and managed to satisfy the need I had to kill. Time was flying, but I wasn't having no damn fun!

Back in my penthouse, I took off my heels and wiggled my way out of my dress on my walk toward the Jacuzzi, planning to soak and get my mind right, in that order. Walking past the spot where I'd left a dead mark earlier, I felt a smile at my lips as I inhaled the fresh scent of lemon and bleach.

Trading in the soothing style of Mr. Vandross, I put on that old Rick Ross "God Forgives, I Don't," feeling like it fit my mood in every way, and continued preparing myself mentally for the battle that loomed in my immediate future. I finished my blunt and lit another after turning on the good Jacuzzi jets, stopping to admire my reflection in the floor-length mirror.

Having a son did nothing if not make me more voluptuous, spreading my hips and adding more ass to my already-thick five-foot-eight frame. My titties didn't sag, either, which was why I very rarely wore a bra, plus it was a good distraction for women and men alike. My face was flawless, no lines or any other signs of aging and stress, beautiful enough to grace the cover of any magazine.

But so much deaths has left me feeling ugly in a way that neither showers nor baths could erase.

"Enough of this shit," I said, climbing into the tub, grabbing the handheld mirror I stashed out of sight with my ready lines of coke. Finishing up my second blunt, I snorted two lines of the fine crystallized powder, feeling wave after wave of euphoria cascade over me as I let my mind wander off on its own course. Scooting forward to one of the jets pushing water at me, I allowed it to align perfectly with my pussy, and within minutes I feel the release of a much-needed orgasm. Only then did I open all the doors in my mind and see things without gray areas, just the black and white of death and destruction.

It was two hours before I was able to pull myself out of my self-induced coma, accepting that I couldn't prolong the inevitable. Back in my closet, I grabbed a pair of all-black cargo pants, a black long-sleeved shirt, my bulletproof vest, and a pair of old-school black Timbs. This was back to the basic wear, the shit most muthafuckas on a come-up in any ghetto wore, because it was common knowledge that being in all-black guaranteed you were on some other shit.

I dressed quickly, pulling the last strap tight on my belt when I hear the doorbell ringing insistently. Going to my bedside table, I scanned all the cameras surrounding my building, the alleys behind it, and the buildings across from it, but I didn't detect a threat. At my front door was my head of security, my second in charge, and my son, but the sight of him was enough to have me already moving toward the door, slipping my gun up out of my purse on the way.

"What's wrong?" I asked, throwing the door open, catching my son as he leapt into my arms and buried his head in my neck. "Tay, what's wrong? Are you hurt?" I asked frantically, searching him while I made my way with him to the couch to sit down. "Baby, talk to me. What is it?" But still he said nothing, just held onto me tighter and tighter.

I looked at my people, my eyes demanding answers in that terrified panic that grips every parent at the moment even closely resembling this. "Talk."

"We, uh, we don't know how it happened, but him and Vita got snatched during the game."

I couldn't have heard him right, so I shook my head and waited for the ringing to stop. "Say what?"

"Somehow, someone abducted him and Vita, Ms. Keyz."

Everything around me turned red and bordered on fading to black, but I bit my tongue to stave off the faint that was coming. Gangstas don't faint. "Are you telling me that someone had my son? My child?" I ask in the deadliest of whispers. I could see the sweat on both of their flushed faces. It felt like I could hear each individual drop emerge from their pores and start to slide. "Answer me!" I growled, feeling the warmth of death in the air, the taste of its heat on my tongue.

"Ms. Keyz, we had them well guarded, but—"

He never got to finish making that excuse as my gun coughed two bullets into his face and he fell backward through my glass coffee table. I felt Tay tense at the violence going on around him, and I had to make a concerted effort to reel in all the emotions I was currently feeling. I didn't want to harm him more than he already was. God knew what my baby had been through.

"Eternity, we go back a long way, don't we?"

"Yes."

"I took you in after shit got bad in Virginia, and I promised you vengeance for the murder of your mother, right?"

"Yes."

"And it's because of this shared history that I'm not going to shoot you down like a rabid dog right now. But bitch, if you don't formulate some sentences that make complete sense in the next twenty seconds, I'll blow your muthafuckin' pretty little head off," I said calmly, raising my gun until the barrel was winking at her frightened gray eyes.

"Somebody fucked up, and they were able to capitalize off it. Who they are we still don't know, because he's not talking and there's no sign of Vita. Maybe she was involved."

"I don't want maybes, Eternity," I said through clenched teeth, working extremely hard not to shoot her.

"You want answers, and I would too, but I don't have them because my concern was getting your son back to you. He has the answers you need."

Despite how much I hated to admit it, she was right, because I would have murdered whoever had tried to question my son. He was mine, and someone had done the unforgivable by going after him. There was only one person I could see doing that, but how had she managed it way up here?

"There's one other thing. When we found him at the garden, he had a bag stapled to his back. There was a heart in the bag."

"A heart?" I asked, confused.

"A-a human heart, but we don't know whose."

"Vita's," he whispered into my neck, and I could feel the slow trickle of his tears burning my flesh.

All I could do was close my eyes, and let my gun fall from my grasp to the couch as I held and rocked my baby, his little body shaking with the force of his tears. I couldn't be sure about what he'd seen, but whatever it was he wouldn't soon forget.

Silence ensued as we both wept quietly for different reasons. Him for the destruction he witnessed and the loss of his aunt, me for the same loss, but also the loss of my little boy's innocence.

I open my eyes, and the look I turned on Eternity was one of concentrated fury. "I'm going to Virginia. You need to make the necessary preparations for that trip, as well as putting in place a team of no less than fifty guards for my son immediately. I want guards guarding my son until we find out just how it was that my security team was breached so successfully. You best find the answer to that question, Eternity, because I swear to you I will personally execute every employee on my staff, including you. Understand?"

"Yes."

"Until you have those answers, I strongly suggest you don't let me see your face. Leave me."

Without a word, she spun on her heels, her phone already at her ear doing whatever was necessary to save her life. My mind was completely focused on revenge, and the thoughts of it were so delicious that I felt my pussy get wet, but first things first, I had to tend to the most important man in my life.

"Baby? Baby, I need to talk to you," I told him, pulling him around until he was sitting on my lap and I could look down into his chocolate-colored eyes. What I saw broke my heart. So much pain, so much understanding, so much like his daddy. "Sweetheart, I want you to listen to me, okay? No one, no one will ever hurt you again, and that's a promise that I'm making you right now on my life. You know I love you, right? Right, Tay?"

"Yeah."

"Then I need you to trust me, baby, and know that I'd rather die than let anything happen to you, ever!"

"But I don't want you to die, Mommy," he whispered, tears filling his still-swimming eyes and following the same beaten path down his young face.

"You don't have to worry about that, baby, because I'm gonna be here for a long time," I told him, giving the best smile I could manage. "I need you to tell me what happened, baby, whatever you can remember. Take your time."

He didn't speak, didn't even look at me anymore, but had his hands clasped firmly in his lap. His silence was so loud, but I knew I had to let him work through this at his own speed in his own way. My stomach is already doing flips, not knowing what to expect or how bad my little boy has been damaged by all that'd happened so far. He was still staring at his hands, but I could feel him thinking, and I knew his little mind was seeing things I never wished for him to know existed.

His first words startled, and then pierced me to my core. "Aunt Vita loves you, Mommy. She told me that before– before the woman cut her neck."

A million questions ran through my mind, but I asked none of them as I took in the knowledge that my son saw someone he loves executed in an intimate and brutal fashion. There were no words to describe how much I ached for what he'd gone through, and sadly I knew there was more to the story.

"She– she didn't want me to see her die, but the lady did. Aunt Vita told me to look away, but. But I couldn't, Mom. It didn't seem real," he whispered, taking my hand in his own and holding it tightly.

Innocence. She had stolen my baby's innocence. I felt the familiar heat of rage creeping through my body, but I checked it for the moment so I could be Mommy right now. "What else happened, baby?"

"The woman, she– she told me to tell you what happened, and to show you my back."

"Your back? What about your back?" I asked, quickly removing him from my lap and stripping his jersey off. What I saw was like a cold bucket of reality that froze my blood and confirmed what I knew the truth to be. In black marker, a simple warning was written: "Expect no mercy from the hands of those you betray!" I couldn't remember the last time I'd known real fear, but I felt it now when I thought about what could've happened to my little boy, my everything. He could've died, and his blood would've been all on my hands, my conscience. I'd rather die a thousand times than ever have to shoulder that burden.

Holding my son tighter, I picked him up and took him into the bathroom across from his room, where I ran him a bath, and gently began scrubbing the words off his back. I didn't speak, and neither did he. We both just tried to forget something that would forever haunt us for different reasons.

As the last of the letters finally came off of his delicate skin, I heard my front door open and the sounds of my army coming in, but I closed the bathroom door, needing the sanctuary that only he could offer for as long as possible. I didn't know what to do without my little man, but I knew what I'd do to prevent ever having to ask myself that question again.

"Baby, listen. I have to go out of town for a couple of days, but I will be back as soon as I can. Don't worry."

"I know you have to go home."

"You do?"

"The woman said you would, but that she hoped you wouldn't."

"What else did she say?" I asked warily.

"Lots of stuff," he replied, developing a sudden fascination with the bubbles surrounding him.

"Lots of stuff like what, Devonte?"

"About— about how she loves my daddy, and that's why she wouldn't hurt me. Mom, who's my daddy?"

Chapter Thirteen

I envisioned this conversation five or hopefully ten years down the line, but not now, not today. Where did I even begin to tell the story? I could feel the stare of his inquisitive eyes on me, but now it was I who couldn't look at him, because I was scared he'd see right through me.

"Mom?"

"Your daddy. Your daddy is someone I've loved my whole life. He was a good man. The best I've ever known."

"Did he love you?"

"Yeah, he did."

"Did he love me?"

"He loves you right now, sweetheart," I say, picking him up out of the tub and sitting him on my lap, oblivious to him getting me all wet.

"But I thought she said my daddy died."

"That doesn't mean he can't still love you from heaven, baby."

"So Daddy's in heaven?"

"If heaven has a ghetto, you can believe that your dad is up there running things," I replied, smiling genuinely for the first time in a long time.

"How did my Daddy die, Mom?"

Wow. That was the million-dollar question I was waiting for, and I still wasn't prepared for how hard it hit me. "What did she say?"

"She told me to ask you."

How decent of her, I thought sarcastically, but it really was. "We'll talk about it when you're older."

"Mom!"

"Devonte, don't push it. Now take this towel, go in your room, and put your nightclothes on."

Without further argument, he slipped from my lap and wrapped his little body in the towel I handed him, obviously not satisfied, but smart enough to know when to leave well enough alone. For now.

"Hey, Tay?" I called as he opened the door. "Did she say what her name was?"

He shook his head and continued on into the hallway, but then he stopped and came back. "She said I was her stepson."

And in that statement, a big piece of the puzzle slid into place and a lot of questions were answered. Nodding my head, I got up and headed back into the living room where I found at least seventy of my best soldiers talking amongst themselves and passing blunts. I easily spotted Eternity in the crowd and summoned her with a nod.

"I said fifty."

"I know, but when word got out about Tay, a few volunteered. He's a Blood drop all the way."

I understood that in a way that no one else could since the secret of who his Daddy is was one that was closely guarded. "Listen, run the names of all Italians we have on the payroll, all the way down to the muthafuckas washing cars."

"And then what?"

"Kill 'em all," I replied casually and walked to where I could be heard and seen by all in the room. "Listen up. No one person is bigger than this nation, so let me be the first to admit that I've been slippin'. That ends now. I've been Keyz for a long time, but it's time for muthafuckas to get familiar with this almighty Blood storm, feel me? We're at war, plain and simple. There is no peace talks, and motherfuck a prisoner. Through death is the only way we'll realize peace. Our enemies are bitches, literally, but not ones we can take lightly, as their tutor was one of our own: my big brother. One is his widow, who is responsible for my son and Vita being kidnapped, because she's turned into the spaghetti-slurping grease balls up here. The other is my brother's mistress, and while the two make an unlikely pair, trust me, they are lethal. Combined, they managed to take over the better part of a $600,000,000 empire that our blood, sweat, and tears helped build. Well, tonight we began to take back what's ours, dig me? I've got someone on the inside, and we're gonna get their base of operations as soon as it gets dark, which means we need to get on the road ASAP. Any questions?"

"Yeah," Eternity said, coming to stand before me.

"What?"

"I thought the soldiers would stay here to protect Tay?"

"Change of plans. I'ma hide my son in the last spot anyone would think to look for him, but once we get there, fifty soldiers will stay there."

"Okay."

"Squad up, we leave in twenty minutes."

Going back to my son's room, I grab a bag from his closet and start filling it with toys and clothes. "Where am I going, Mommy?"

"Somewhere safe, baby."

"Will you come back to get me?"

His question stopped me cold once again, forcing me to acknowledge his newfound knowledge of the real things that go bump in the night. One look in his eyes showed clearly his fear of losing me, but I wondered if he could see the same in my eyes.

Setting the bag down, I go and squat in front of where he sits on his bed. Gently, I take his face in my hands until I'm staring so deeply into his eyes that I'm watching his life story unfold as if I didn't live it with him.

"Baby, I want you to listen to me. No matter what, I'm not gonna leave you or lose you. I know a terrible thing happened today, and now I have to go make sure it won't happen again, but nothing, *nothing* is more important to me than being your Mommy. Okay?"

"Okay," he replied, hugging me fiercely and then going to pick up his bag so he could pack the things he liked most. I smiled. He was independent and determined, my qualities as much as his dad's.

Twenty minutes later, the packing was done, the guns were loaded, and my fifteen-car caravan was moving with the purpose of straight destruction. My son slept with his head in my lap, and I gently rubbed his scalp, praying that sweet dreams would come instead of the nightmares so often following trauma.

Eternity rode in the car with us, but she didn't speak, only stared out at the passing highways when she was not texting a mile a minute. Her day for revenge had been long coming, too, and looking at her closer, I could see how much the last five years have aged her. She was still beautiful by any standards with her penetrating gray eyes, mocha-brown skin, long black hair, and delicious curves, but I could see a hardness about her now. Before her mother was killed, her beauty had been almost delicate, even if she was anything other than, but now I could see the roads she'd traveled in the redness of her eyes and the slight creases in her brow from lack of smiles. What did she have to smile about?

I wanted to smoke, but not with my little man this close to me. The stress of indecision was actually causing me to crave the feeling of being high. My main concern wasn't the impending battle, it was Devonte's safety. He was all I had in this world, and I couldn't be sure that giving him to her was a smart decision, but it was a safe one.

Closing my eyes, I let the soothing ride of my car lull me into a light sleep, coming completely alert when we stopped in front of the all-white townhouse. The sun was setting behind it. It looked the same as it had five years ago, except far more flowers and the money-green Mercedes E Class parked in the driveway.

"You want me to take him in?" Eternity asked.

Part of me did. Part of me didn't want to face this woman whose life I had forever changed and was about to change again. I had to, though. "No, I got it," I said, scooping up the still-sleeping little boy in my arms and stepping out into the cool summer air when my door was opened.

I quickly walked to the door and rang the bell before I lost my nerve. I heard movement inside, and then I came face-to-face with the woman indirectly responsible for my son.

"Yes? Kiara, is that you?"

"Yes, ma'am."

"Well, come in. You just gonna stand on my front stoop?" she replied, leading the way into the house and further into the den. "Whose little boy is that?" she asked.

"He's mine."

"I never even knew you were pregnant. How old is he?"

"He's five."

"Five? And you're just now bringing him to see me?" she asked, obviously irritated and hurt.

"I'm sorry, Ms. Mitchell, life has been crazy. After Devaughn died, I just kind of…."

"I understand, baby. It was hard on me, too. My son wasn't perfect, but he was mine. As a mother, I'm sure you know exactly how I feel."

I couldn't utter a word or a sound, afraid my voice would betray me. I couldn't even look her in the eye for fear of her seeing my truth and never being able to understand or forgive me. I had to get out of here. "Listen, Ms. Mitchell, I know this is beyond short notice, but I have some important business to handle and, well, there's no one I trust him with except you."

She looked at me, then to my little boy still sleeping in my arms, and back to me. I wondered if she could see it, her son in mine. Maybe not while he slept, but it was undeniable once he was awake.

She gave me a slow nod, and I sat down on the couch, putting Devonte on his feet to wake him up. "Tay, wake up, baby."

"Hmm?"

"Listen, I'm leaving you here with family, and don't worry, because you're safe. I want you to do everything she tells you, okay?"

"Okay, Mommy."

"Now give me a hug and a kiss so I can go."

He complied with my request, but I could tell how hard it was to let me go. It was one of the hardest things I'd ever done.

Kissing him quickly, I headed for the door before my heart overrode my mind. Opening the door, I grabbed his bag off the stoop and turned around in time to hear a sharp intake of breath from inside the house. One look at Devaughn's mother's face told me that she'd seen the truth, and the look she gave me was full of questions without answers. Giving her a sad smile, I pulled the front door closed, ran to my car, and hopped in, only then releasing the breath I'd been holding.

"Fifty soldiers strong, and twenty with us," I told Eternity, lighting a blunt as she stepped out of the car to make the arrangements. Within minutes she was back, and we were on our way, traveling roads as familiar to me as they were alien.

Inside of an hour, we reached the edge of my property, facing the back of my estate. I hadn't laid eyes on this house in over five years, but memories came flooding back as if I'd never been away, and the taste of betrayal was heavy on my tongue. Lifting my phone, I hit redial and waited for an answer.

"I'm here."

"Hey, sweetheart, we are just sitting down for dinner."

"Who's there?"

"I'm sorry I couldn't call you back earlier, but I've been spending the afternoon with all my sisters and a new friend. As soon as I help Mona and Candy put little DJ to bed, I'll be over, okay?"

"Did you handle the lights?"

"Yep, everything is great."

"I'm on the way in."

"Okay, see you soon."

Disconnecting the call. I tucked my phone back in my pocket and prepared to address my team. Motioning with my hands, I gathered everyone around so I could speak as quietly as possible. "A'ight, listen, there's only eight people in there, not counting staff. One is a child and one a friend, so we try to avoid killing them. The light-skin bitch with dreads and the Spanish-looking bitch with curly black hair are the primary targets, so do not miss them. Shoot on sight. We got the element of surprise, so this shit shouldn't be hard. Just don't get careless. Any questions?" No one spoke, but I hadn't actually expected them to. It was time for action. "Load up."

Going to my trunk, I pulled out a beautiful black Mac 2, checking to make sure the clip was full and the first bullet was ready to party. Next, I put on a shoulder holster where I put my fully-loaded 9mm and tucked it next to a clip for each weapon in my pockets. The sound of bullets sliding into chambers was the only sound in the night. Even the insects hushed when death spread its wings.

Once my team was ready, I took off at a steady jog, angling toward the house, but staying out of sight of the cameras I knew were on each end. I hesitated for only a second once I got within range of the motion sensors, but when they didn't go off, I resumed my cautious pace until we were right up on the patio. Signaling again with my hands, I waited as Eternity opened the outside power box and prepared to kill the lights. Game face on, gun in my hands, I let all the anger, rage, fear, and pain flood my body until all I could see, all I could smell, was death.

And then I gave a nod.

The lights went out, and death darkened the door of my house once again.

Chapter Fourteen

Deshana

I had to admit, it felt good to be back home. Not necessarily back in this house, but back in the streets where I'd grown up for so long, surrounded by so much love and acceptance. My little brother DJ was just the cutest thing. He was a miniature version of our Pops, from his looks to his humor. I loved him already. He was entertaining everyone now as we ate dinner, talking about all the little girls in his kindergarten class. He was definitely my father's son!

I could tell JuJu was enjoying herself. Home girl had become all smiles since we got on the helicopter at the airport, teasing me about being rich this whole time. Money did make shit easier, but some things even money couldn't buy or fix.

I felt Jordyn's eyes on me again. I swear the girl had been trying to stare a fucking hole through me since I got there. Five years had changed her a lot. She'd bloomed into an attractive woman in a lot of ways. Her ass filled out, along with the infamous titties we all got from our mom, but she had more of Mom's caramel skin tone than I did. I was chocolate, like my daddy, and proud of it. She was taller than me now, putting her at least at five-foot-five, probably weighing about 135 pounds. Her face was okay. It would probably even be beautiful once she stopped getting pimples. Or maybe she just needed some dick. She was tense as hell.

La-La and Day-Day looked exactly the same. Day-Day was a little taller than me, but we were the same weight and complexion. La-La looked more like Mommy every day, but she had a professional air to the honey-toned, loud-mouthed beauty that she used to be.

Looking at Candy and Mona, I could tell that these last five years had been more than difficult. Both had lines on their beautiful faces one could attribute to stress, age, or both. Candy's dreads were down to her ass, but they couldn't hide how thick she was. She was easily model material as a complete package, except for her height, because she was only around four-foot-eleven in sneakers.

Mona had that movie-star beauty, but I could expect no less since she was half Dominican and half Italian. If I didn't love her, I'd hate her. I was worried about her, though, because her eyes were taking on that yellowish tone that came from too much smoking, and that wasn't her style.

The ringing phone interrupted me analyzing those surrounding me, and what I heard in Jordyn's voice had my antennas on the rise. She actually sounded happy. I wondered who the caller was. She'd been so sullen ever since I got back that I thought she was going through her stubborn teen mosh-pit phase, albeit late in life. It seemed I wasn't the only one surprised, though, because La-La and Day-Day were discreetly paying attention, too. And at the mention of DJ's name, Candy and Mona became intrigued by the conversation.

When she hung up, a hush suddenly seemed to come over the table, except for little DJ, who was enjoying his fifteen minutes of fame.

"You wanna help put DJ to bed?" Candy asked, and the way she asked the question made it clear that this wasn't a first-time thing. It was definitely usual.

"Sure," Jordyn replied. "Doesn't he look sleepy?"

This brought immediate protest from DJ, who hated bedtime with the same passion of all children his age, but I was in agreement with him, because he didn't look the least bit sleepy.

"Calm down, DJ, you're not going to bed," Mona told him, sliding a glance at Jordyn, who looked like she wanted to say something or offer some objection. I couldn't understand why. I mean, if she had somewhere to be, she could easily leave.

Other conversations started back up, but I could feel something in the air that didn't sit right with me. My father had given me a love for old-school hip-hop, so it was no surprise to me when Blaine Sigel's song "Feel It in the Air" popped into my mind. He never lied when he said eighty-five percent of communication was non-verbal, because Jordyn's body language was screaming that something was all the way wrong. La-La and Day-Day were oblivious, and Candy was putting more food on DJ's plate. Mona seemed to be in her own thoughts, but when I looked down the table to my left, I could see JuJu was vibin' with me as always.

"What's up Ju?" I asked nonchalantly.

"Nothin' much. I smell two hundred, though."

To this statement I raised a quizzical eyebrow, because what she was saying didn't make sense. Two hundred was the code for blood or death. In response to my look, she gave me a slight nod, but I didn't need to look in that direction because I could feel those eyes on me again. "Let's take a walk real quick, Ju—"

I didn't get to finish the sentence before my peripheral vision caught the movement and the sound of a safety being taken off reached my ears. I didn't move. I didn't even blink as I stared across the table at my baby sister, who was pointing a mean-looking Ruger p229 at me.

Silence filled the room. Even my little brother was smart enough to shut up when guns and bullets were on the dessert menu.

"Jordyn, what the fuck?"

"Shut up, Latavia. This is between me and that bitch."

"That bitch is your sister, or have you forgotten that along with losing the rest of your damn mind?"

"She ain't my sister. She's a murdering piece of shit like her rapist daddy!"

I felt my blood pumping and the adrenaline start to flow, but the rage that came wasn't white hot as most tended to be. It was cold, ice cold, and working its way around my heart until it wasn't a sister I saw in front of me. She was a dead bitch holding a gun.

"Put the gun down, J-baby, and talk."

"Don't call me no fucking J-baby! He gave me that fucking name like he loved me, but he let his daughter murder my father in cold blood. For nothing!" she screamed, shaking so hard that I didn't know if I would be shot in my face or chest. The scarier part was that I didn't care because all I needed was a moment, just one moment, and I'd reunite father and daughter.

"Who told you she killed your father?" Candy asked, speaking for the first time, but she knew like I knew. That secret could only come from one person.

"Keyz said."

At that instant the power went out and I made my move, rolling to my left until I felt a bullet rip through my shoulder and send me sprawling over the chair. Pushing through the pain, I continued to roll, trying my best to move out of the way of Jordyn's reckless shots, but I could hear the bullets dancing all around me. Luckily, Candy had provided me with a few pistols, and I saw JuJu laying down cover fire as I pulled my own .357 out and let it bark behind me.

Scrambling to my feet, I saw JuJu right in front of me but I felt the double tap of bullets as I got hit in my back and I was suddenly falling into her arms.

My last thoughts were a question of what my dad would look like when I saw him.

***

Ramona

I couldn't believe what the fuck I was seeing, but I knew it was true. Little Jordyn was actually pointing a loaded pistol at her own sister with complete hatred in her eyes. I knew how we'd all missed it before because we simply weren't around each other, but how did we not see it this evening before this?

Her anger and pain were so raw, the emotions contorted her entire face into a mask fit for demons. She wouldn't be dissuaded or talked down. She meant to spill blood. She meant to kill Deshana, but why?

No sooner had I asked, the answer was spoken, and I had a sudden flash of clarity about this whole situation. I knew Keyz would come. How could she not? But I didn't know she'd actually try us here on our own turf. She may have felt like she had the upper hand in the form of Jordyn, but it was still clear she was operating off unchecked emotions. That was a mistake, and a costly one, too.

Keeping my eyes firmly fixed on Jordyn, I slowly tapped the button under the table in front of me that released the Israeli-made, fully-automatic AK 47 into my waiting hands. No safety and no need to cock it. My father didn't believe in those two aspects of weaponry, and I learned the tricks of the trade at his feet.

Locking eyes with Candy, I nodded toward DJ, my meaning clear. I saw the love she had for both of us come through loud and clear in the look she gave, but just as quickly she tucked it away and prepared to do what was necessary.

I flicked my eyes back to Jordyn just as the lights went out and she opened fire on Deshana. Pushing back from the table, I leveled the barrel of my weapon at her as I put myself between her, DJ, and Candy. Once Candy grabbed DJ and made a break for the panic room under the stairs, I gave Jordyn my full attention just as she put two more rounds into Deshana's back and she collapsed on top of JuJu. The AK sang when I tapped the trigger, making lunchmeat of Jordyn's left arm while her screams pierced the night.

Even though the only light filtering in was from the window, I still spotted multiple shadows slide quietly into the house through the patio door. "On the floor!" I screamed at Day-Day and La-La, letting the sweet harmony of my guns sing above their heads as two figures dropped and three more took direct hits. I felt a bullet lift the curls by my right temple, and I hurriedly put my back to the wall next to the kitchen entrance, which momentarily took me out of the line of fire.

Grabbing the Glock .27 off my waist, I slid it to the silhouette I made out as Day-Day crawling toward me. "Shoot what moves," I told her, finally hearing the ding of the elevator, which meant the guards had arrived. Taking advantage of the distraction, I stepped away from the wall, and me and Day-Day unloaded a sweet duet with unrelenting gunfire until I felt blistering heat penetrate my thigh, and the echo of close-range gunshots reached my ears as I hit the ground. Even in the shadows, I knew it was her creeping toward me, could feel the hatred of her stare penetrating the night.

And I finally let in the fear for my unborn child.

***

Candy

Was this really happening? There was no way little Jordyn was pointing a fucking gun at Deshana. But if she was, it could only mean one thing: Keyz.

I'd caught the strange vibe between Jordyn and Deshana, but thought it was more from the long separation than anything else.

I mean, they were sisters! Sisters bickered and argued, but this was taking shit to a whole new level, and I could only see it escalating that far for one reason: Keyz.

Deshana had tortured and executed Jordyn's father all those years ago, and based on the treatment, one would assume he had it coming, but that meant absolutely nothing when it came to the father's daughter. I knew this from experience, seeing as how my own father was gunned down like garbage over a dice game. The woman responsible had paid with her life. Too bad it had been my own mother.

Thinking of Mother brought me back to my priorities. First and foremost was keeping my little angel straight. I saw the look Mona gave me, and all I could hope was the love I felt was conveyed in the look I returned. Readying myself for whatever, I finally heard Jordyn scream the truth at Deshana.

"Who told you she killed your father?" I asked, my stomach turning, because I knew the answer as much as Deshana knew. There was no more hiding from the truth. Gripping the comforting handle of my .45, I snatched DJ out of his chair when the lights went out and scrambled for the door directly under the staircase while Mona laid down cover, and then heavy fire. I could barely hear DJ's screams over the roaring gunfire, but I knew he was terrified and not hit.

Finally making it to the door, I placed my palm over the scanner and the door slid soundlessly open, revealing a ten-by-twenty room stocked with weapons, food, and cameras surveying our property. "Go, DJ," I said, putting him on his feet and grabbing the 12-gauge Mossberg sitting up against the wall.

"Mom!"

I heard him scream, but I'd already hit the button to reseal the room, and my mind was centered on one thing: Keyz.

I heard and saw Mona letting that AK work its magic on the muthafuckas who crept in the back door, and after tucking the .45

in my jeans, I let my Mossberg roar out a nice hello myself, relishing the sight of a man leaving his feet. The fragrance of gun smoke filled my nostrils and wet my appetite for vengeance, giving me pleasure that was almost orgasmic while I let off shot after shot. Steadily working my way back toward Mona, I saw JuJu crawl from underneath Deshana, but she never left her side as she emptied her clip at the shadows trying to advance.

To my left, I heard a grunt of pain, and I looked over in time to see Mona falling to the floor, grabbing her legs tight. I felt my heart hit my stomach, and it was hard to breathe for a minute. And even as I took in the hurt of my lover, my friend being shot, it still didn't compare to the horrific smile stretching through the darkness that belonged to her shooter.

It had been five long years of pain laced with desire. Five years of anguish and anticipation. Five years of remembering all this bitch had stolen from me, and now here she was, trying to repeat the cycle.

"Not this time, bitch," I mumbled, catching her profile with the full blast of my shotgun, sending her flying through the swinging kitchen door.

Quickly making my way to Mona, I checked to make sure there was nothing injured except her leg, then pulled my t-shirt off and tightly tied it around the wound.

"Candy, I'm. I'm."

"Shh, I gotta get you to the panic room."

"Keyz."

"That bitch ain't going nowhere. I just hit her with the shotty. Don't talk. Grab that chopper and cover us while I drag you," I told her, grabbing her under her arms and pulling her as quickly as I could without hurting her.

As we neared Deshana, I saw her stumbling to her feet with JuJu's help and letting her .357 go for all it was worth. What had started out as an even gunfire was now looking to be one in our favor, because the guards were picking niggas off left and right, exploding Black Talon rounds lighting the way like Christmas trees.

Finally getting to the door, I got it open again and pushed Mona next to a huddled DJ. "Take care of him," I said, slamming my palm on the button and closing the doors on both of their protests.

Pulling the .45, I stepped into the fray, letting my instincts take over completely as I made my way back to the kitchen door. The gun smoke was so thick and stifling that I could barely see across the room with only the moonlight as my guide, but still I dumped slug after slug until the rattling of shells hitting the marble floor sounded like music notes.

I approached the kitchen door cautiously, pushing it wide and stepping back in case of gunfire. When none came, I pulled off the wall and sprung into the room, scanning it quickly and only finding a huge puddle of blood with a trail leading out the back door. I could hear gunfire outside, which meant the bitch was on the run, but I couldn't let her get away. Not this time.

Aryanna

Chapter Fifteen

Deshana

I felt like a blowtorch was being taken to my shoulder, and it was still hard to breathe from where Jordyn's shots had tried to battle through my Teflon vest, but I was alive. And pissed.

Still holding onto JuJu for support, I dropped my now-empty pistol and made my way toward Jordyn's gun, which had slid under the table. Looking for an enemy, any enemy, I took in the room before me with sweeping glances, pistol out front and ready to play tag. I spotted Day-Day in the corner with a pistol in one hand and her other hand clenching La-La's, her frightened expression plain as day even in the moonlight surrounding us.

There were bodies scattered everywhere, none moving, though, and I could still hear major gunshots ringing loudly outside. "Come on, Ju, we gotta help," I said, making toward the patio door only to feel her pulling me to a stop.

"You're bleeding all over the place, and I did not fly three thousand fucking miles to lose you now, so sit it down and let's stop the bleeding."

"But!"

"But ass, bitch, sit down!" she replied, forcefully pushing me down into the chair she'd occupied at dinner. Just the thought of the meal we were sharing seemed far away, like it took place days or even months ago instead of moments.

"I can't see shit in this light!" JuJu complained, causing me to wince as she probed my shoulder for the bullet. "In and out, but we still need to stop the bleeding."

Just then the backup lights kicked on and gave the clarity we needed.

"Day-Day, you and La-La all right?" I asked, fearing shock might be gripping both of them with the way their bodies were shaking.

"Ye-yeah," Day-Day replied, never taking her eyes off the dead bodies or lowering the pistol clenched firmly in her grasp.

The moaning to my right drew my attention, and whom did I find cradling the bloody mess that vaguely resembled an arm? None other than my treacherous sibling. In one stride I was on her, ignoring the pain in my shoulder as my entire body rocked with the force of the blows I was delivering to her face with the pistol. The first blow demolished her nose, the second and third brought the sweet crunching sound of a broken jaw to my ears like a lover's whisper. By the fifth blow, I was estimating that she only had about twelve of her original thirty-two teeth, and I meant to shatter those, too, but I felt JuJu grab me from behind.

"You're gonna bleed out, homey. Let that bitch breathe for a second."

My body was on fire with the need to hurt her. Not simply kill the bitch, but hurt her in the process. But I felt myself weakening, and I knew JuJu was right. "I need a favor, Ju."

"Anything, you know that."

"There's a room one floor below this one. When you get off the elevator, you go to the right, and it's the door at the furthest end. I want you to take her down there and make sure the bitch can't escape, but don't kill her. That's on me."

"Are you going to be all right for a second?"

"Don't start no mother hen shit on me, just handle business," I replied, forcing a smile I didn't feel onto my lips.

She smiled back, but it still didn't mask the worry in her eyes, and I knew if the roles were reversed I'd be the same way. We were sisters, maybe not by blood, but as I just learned the hard way, blood doesn't always come out thicker than water.

JuJu grabbed Jordyn by a fistful of hair and dragged her kicking and mumbling onto the elevator, eventually smacking her across the head with her pistol and knocking her out as they disappeared from sight.

Ramona limped into view, holding an AK, with DJ trailing behind with some towels and other medical supplies in his little arms. Immediately she surveyed the damage, shaking her head, but keeping her thoughts to herself. When her gaze landed on my two sisters in the corner, I could see the concern in her eyes, probably coming to the same conclusion I did.

"Where are you hurt?" she asked, setting her gun down and gently peeling what was left of my t-shirt back.

"Just the shoulder. My vest caught the ones on my back, thankfully. Is your leg okay?"

"Hurts like hell, but I'll live thanks to DJ," she replied, turning a smile in his direction as she took everything she needed from his grasp.

I took his tiny hand in my own, hoping to release him from the fear that I knew had him trapped because of what he'd just witnessed. It was never pretty to have the ugliness of the world touch someone so young and undeserving of it, and I felt for my little brother, knowing just how much he was forever changed.

"Sharday, Latavia, I need your help over here," Mona said, preparing to bandage me up.

At first they didn't move, didn't even seem to hear what Mona had said to them, but slowly Day-Day lowered the pistol and looked in our direction.

"Come here," Mona said impatiently.

Once they were standing beside her, she lowered her voice so DJ wouldn't here, but I still heard her. "I need you two to take care of DJ, because I have to go find Candy. The last time I saw her, she was running away from the back of the estate, shooting, and I have no doubt that it's Kiara in her sights."

"Keyz caused all this?" La-La asked in disbelief.

"Who else? But she made a big miscalculation, and that cost her a lot of men tonight. I won't let it cost me Candy, though, so I need you two, okay?"

"Ramona, go," I said as she finished wrapping and taping my shoulder the best she could.

"Mona!" DJ said when she scooped up her gun and walked to the kitchen door, but she didn't even pause in her stride.

"It's okay, DJ, your big sisters are here with you," I told him, pulling him closer to me and hugging him tightly with my good arm.

"Come on, little man," Day-Day said, handing me her gun in exchange for DJ's hand, and with La-La in tow, she led him toward the stairs. On their way up I heard him ask if he could go see his daddy first, which caused us all to look at each other confused, but Day-Day shook her head anyway and they continued on.

The elevator dinged causing me to grab and raise both pistols, but thankfully it was only my girl Ju, because I doubted my shoulder could stand the recoil from my gunfire.

"Where is everybody?" she asked, sitting next to me.

"My two sisters took my little brother upstairs, and Ramona went to find Candy, who went after Keyz."

"Is this the same Keyz we're here for?"

"None other."

"Wish I could've met the bitch face-to-face, or bullet-to-face. So what's the deal with the one I took downstairs?"

Where should I begin with that story? It seemed like so long ago when I'd murdered her father. Killing him almost seemed insignificant now, though it hadn't been at the time. At the time, he needed killing. "When my dad came home, my mom was with Jordyn's father. They had been off and on for years. I'd never understood why, because he was nothing like my dad, but she kept him around and let him treat her like shit. He beat her, he cheated on her. He even beat us. I didn't know how to deal with my mom letting some nigga abuse her because she'd always taught us to be strong black women, taking no shit from no man. Yet here she was, allowing herself to be treated like nothing. It was her choice, but when she let that piece of shit abuse us, I made the choice that the first chance I got, he'd pay for it. And he did."

There was more to say, more to the story, but even if I wanted to tell it I couldn't, because Mona was bounding back through the doors with tears streaming from her eyes.

"What?" I asked, praying it wasn't what I thought it would be.

"Candy. Candy just got arrested."

"What?" I replied, shock taking the place of worry and relief entering my bloodstream a little. It was only then my subconscious linked with my conscious and I heard the sound of sirens in the not-too-far distance.

"When I got to the edge of the property, I saw Candy handcuffed in the back of a cop car, and there was a woman's body in the street. I don't know if it was Keyz or not, but they've got Candy, and it ain't good."

My mind was racing, but going nowhere. Shit had gone from bad to worse to completely fucked up, and that was still an understatement!

"Do either of you have warrants?"

Ju and I just looked at each other, both of us thinking about the very public execution I'd committed earlier today. "I don't know, why?"

"Because it is only a matter of time before the cops get here, Deshana. Y'all gotta hide. Go downstairs into the—"

"Mona!" DJ hollered from upstairs somewhere.

"In a minute, DJ. Look, you know the room where—"

"Mona!" DJ yelled again, this time chilling my blood, because it was evident something wasn't right with him.

Mona sensed it, too. I could tell by the way her body language changed and she raised her gun again. "Yeah, DJ?" she asked, moving to the bottom of the stairs, careful not to make herself too much of a target.

"Daddy wants you and Mommy!"

"Your daddy. Your daddy? What?" she replied, turning an almost sickly color white in her face.

"Daddy wants you and Mommy!" he shouted again, his voice fading as he moved off into another part of the house.

"Oh, God," she murmured, dropping her gun and taking the stairs two at a time.

I didn't understand what was going on or how a dead man could want, but I pushed myself out of the chair so JuJu and I could follow. Once we reached the top the stairs, I was lost as to which way to go until I heard a scream that raised the hair on my arms and had me running after it. I rounded the corner and came to an upstairs library, which had an open hidden panel. Gun out in front of me, I crept slowly into the hidden space, coming out into a smaller library where I found DJ, Mona, Day-Day, and La-La standing in front of a chair.

"What the fuck, y'all?" I asked, upset that they scared the shit out of me, but nobody seemed to be dead or in danger of dying.

No one spoke. No one moved. And then, one by one, they stepped back to show me what they were so fucked up about. Sitting in a brown leather chair, just as calm as you please, was the first man I'd ever loved in my entire life. But how was that possible?

"Da-Da-Daddy?" I whispered, but I never heard his response as darkness closed in and welcomed me to some much-needed rest.

Chapter Sixteen

Keyz

God, the pain in my arm was excruciating! So much blood. Could I be dying? Is that what it felt like? How the fuck had things gone so terribly wrong? From the moment Eternity killed the power and I heard gunshots, I knew that stupid bitch Jordyn had jumped the gun, but still our numbers should have made up for that. And yet there I was, fleeing again with my arm damn near falling off my body.

A lot of the shotgun's blast had been absorbed by my vest, thankfully, but that muthafucka still packed a punch like nothing I'd ever experienced. I was so focused on Ramona, tasting her death for what she's done to my son and Vita, so eager that I didn't pay close enough attention to my surroundings, and now it might have cost me my life.

Devonte. What about my baby? How could I leave him alone in this world? I felt the tears rolling down my cheeks faster and faster and felt the wails of agony working their way up from my stomach, and not caring who heard me, I let them out.

"We're almost to the hospital, Keyz!" I heard someone yell from the front seat of my speeding car, but they couldn't understand that my pain was deeper than the bleeding wounds or that of my injured pride. My baby was all I had left in this world, and I wasn't ready to leave him.

I could feel my heartbeat slowing, and then I felt a chill I'd only had described to me before by one person. I wondered if he'd be there to meet me on the other side. Would he love me, or at least understand how I came to love him so much? Would what I felt finally be accepted because we were beyond the rules of here and now? I found comfort in just the thought of going with him again. Even though I didn't want to leave my son, being with his father was a blessing in itself.

Everything felt like it was underwater or in slow motion as my car slid to a stop and I felt hands lifting me. And then came the pain.

"Ah, shit! My fucking arm!"

"You're at the hospital, Keyz, just hold on."

Surrounding me were nurses, other people, sick people. It smelled like death was closing in on me. I was put on a gurney that felt more like a roller coaster and sent flying down a hall until I came to a halt behind some double doors. It was hard to breathe, my arm hurt so bad, but if I could feel it, I guessed that meant I wasn't dead yet. Maybe it wasn't my time.

I felt the prick of a needle in my good arm, followed momentarily by the blissful sensation of some good drugs navigating their way through my bloodstream. It made me feel light and far away from the beeping and hissing of the machines I was being hooked up to. My eyes felt like weightlifters, grumbling under too much strain, and I had no inclination to fight them when they fell.

I was asleep, but I wasn't. How would I know? Because I was still very much aware of where I was and what had landed me there, but on the back of my eyelids played movies from my past. I saw myself as a nine-year-old little girl, very country in my pigtails and overalls, but that was the fashion at the time in Alabama. I saw myself looking at the one picture my dad had of Devaughn. I thought he was about fourteen in it, but even then he was handsome in his own way, and I could see the intelligence in his eyes as well as the mischief.

Like a kaleidoscope, the image changed until I was reading the first letter he ever wrote me from prison, even though I couldn't yet comprehend why he was there or what it all meant. It didn't matter what he did, he was my big brother, and I loved him. After our dad died, me and my sister, Keisha, moved to Virginia to live with our other half-brother and his wife, which excited me, because I was now in the same state as Devaughn, therefore destined to meet. I could see myself sitting nervously in the visiting room, waiting on him to walk through the doors, but scared too, because I didn't know what to expect, what to think, or what to want.

And then it happened. He breezed into the room, larger than life, giving head nods and occasional smiles to those he passed, and I could see the respect he commanded as well as the fear. I was far from a woman, and my body was still a curiosity to me, but the throbbing of my young pussy accompanied by the moisture I felt was as clear a sign as I'd ever seen. I wanted him. This wasn't my half brother. This wasn't a sibling I grew up with. This was a man who emitted feral power in a way I'd never known. But he wasn't just *a* man. He was *the* man.

If I was asked to repeat the conversation held that afternoon, I couldn't, not a word of it, but I could remember how he made me feel completely and utterly special. He didn't simply hear what I said, he listened, and it was evidenced by his responses and his eye contact. God, was his eye contact amazing! Too soon it was over, and I was reduced to tears, but then he did something I was not soon to forget, something that kept both my mind and my fingers at work for years to come. He kissed my tears away.

From that moment onward, I knew he'd never be a brother to me. He had to be everything, because there was no way there was another nigga like him. No way! From then on, we exchanged letters like new friends, and then old friends, until we became best friends. I loved him and he loved me, even if he couldn't see or understand how deep his love went for me. He didn't treat me as a little kid. He wasn't condescending, because we were equals, and he taught me the things I needed to know about life and death. And together we grew. I didn't fall in love with him, I grew in love with him, and he looked after me like I was one of his own, because I was.

Again the imagery broke up, and I saw the first day he came home, felt that swell of love stir within me all over again at the feel of his arms around me when we hugged. He was home, and he was mine. Or he should've been, but I'd fucked up and brought Candy into the picture. She couldn't love him like me. No one could.

I could see the night I made love to him, the night he gave me the precious gift of his seed and made me complete in a way no one would ever take from me. I could smell his scent, still feel his dick in my tight pussy, and even now I felt that heat steadily rising, steadily building until....

"Child, you okay?"

My images were shattered and reality was back with a swift jolt of pain accompanying it. Not simply the pain in my arm, the deeper pain that slowly caressed my heart. All the years had returned, too, and I already missed whatever plain or state of being I just came from.

"Kiara?"

Her voice caused me to turn my head to my right, where I found her sitting next to my hospital bed, her face illuminated only a little by the dim light burning by my bedside. "Hmm?" I murmur in response, not entirely trusting my voice, despite the fact that we were alone.

"How do you feel, child?"

"I've been better, Ms. M."

"Obviously, baby, but the way you was just moaning and carrying on, I thought you were having some type of relapse. Or erotic dream."

I was glad she couldn't see me blush, because I knew my honey complexion was heating up. "What time is it?" I croaked out, gratefully accepting the glass of water she held as the straw slipped in between my lips and relief found my throat.

"A little before 4:00 a.m. You were in surgery for about five hours. You'd lost a lot of blood."

"My arm?" I asked, trying to lift it, but only succeeding in wiggling my fingers.

"They saved it, but the baby. It was too much."

"What baby?" I demanded, fear knifing through my heart at the thought of losing my little boy again.

"You didn't know you were pregnant?" she asked, obviously confused.

"Pregnant? No. No, I didn't know that. Are you sure?" I asked, wondering when I'd been that careless with Mark and why I didn't feel a bigger sense of loss.

"That's what the doctor said, sweetie. I'm sorry."

"It's. I'm okay. How did you know I was here, and where is Devonte?"

"Well, your *friends* came to my house after they dropped you off here and told me you'd been shot. I don't know if they expected me to give up your son, but that wasn't something I was prepared to do. Right now he's still at my house with my good friend Mr. Woots, sleeping and getting the rest his young body needs."

"He's safe?"

"Do you even need to ask me that, Kiara?"

"I'm sorry, you're right."

"So. Who's his daddy?"

"Do you even need to ask me that?"

"No, I guess not. The better question is how, but please spare me the details of the act itself, because I remember how that goes."

What could I say? How would I say it? I mean, this was Devaughn's mother! The answer was simple: life. "Our child was created in love. No matter how forbidden it may have seemed, it was still love by any measure."

I could see her chewing on my words, digesting them, or maybe she was dissecting them. But either way, no one was there to contest what I was saying.

"Love, huh? Well, Kiara, I know my son, and I know he loved you, but only you would know how much and in what ways. Twenty years in prison changed him in ways I can't imagine, and even though I was there for him, there was only so much I could do. However it turned out, I'm grateful for my grandson, so I guess I'm thanking you for loving my son that much."

The heaviness of guilt pushed the tears from my eyes. I had taken from her more than I could ever give back, and here she was thanking me like I'd done this great favor or service. How was that possible? How had I ended up in this situation?

Before I could say anything, two of my top lieutenants came through my hospital room door. "Keyz, we've got a problem."

"What?"

"Cops. They're on their way up here, but the nurses are stalling because you just got out of surgery."

My mind started racing. It was procedure to report all gunshot victims, and I had absolutely no way of explaining what had happened to me, because the truth was definitely out of the question. "Fairfax County PD?"

"Yeah."

"Shit! Alright, look, I'ma play sleep, and as soon as they leave, we're gone with the wind, got me? Go get the car."

They left quickly, once again making it just the two of us and the huge ghost of the man we loved for company.

"What are you going to do?" she asked, concerned.

"Run. I can't explain this, and I make too much of an easy target if my enemies know where to find me. Can you look after Devonte for a while?"

"Are we back to asking stupid questions again?"

My hospital door swung suddenly opened again, and I snapped my eyes shut.

"Ms. Briggs?"

"She's resting," I heard her reply.

"I'm Detective Robinson, and this is Detec—"

"Your names won't change the fact that she's resting, so you can come introduce yourself later."

"Resting? Then who were you just talking to?"

"It's called prayer, and if you must know, I was communing with God. Is there a law against that?"

"I'm sorry, who are you?" he asked, impatiently stepping further into the room.

"A card-carrying NRA member, a taxpaying citizen, and an old-school bitch that you don't wanna fuck with. Now I kindly suggest you come back at a better time, and understand that this will be the last kind thing I say to you."

I'd never wanted to laugh so hard in my damn life, but I knew I had to keep a straight face or get ready to spend some time in jail.

"We'll, uh. We'll be around, so be sure to let us know when she wakes up," he replied, trying to invoke some authority into his voice.

"Be sure? Negro, please! Get. The fuck. Out!" she hissed at them, rising from her seat and making her way toward them.

I heard the door open and close, and then a sigh of relief. "That was kinda of fun," she said, sitting on the edge of my bed and taking my weakened hand in hers.

"I can tell you enjoyed yourself. Thank you, Ms. M."

"No sweat, baby. And since you've made me a grandma again, I guess it's okay for you to call me Gladys."

I smiled. It was strange, because I didn't know that I still remembered how to do that, but in that moment with that woman, I felt myself simply breathing again. And it felt good.

"So, where will you go? Who are you fighting, baby?"

"I–I can't tell you that, Ms. Gladys, but I'm not going far. I have a lot of business to tend to down here, and I can't think about returning to New York until it's complete."

"Well, be safe then, Kiara. I may be Devonte's grandmother, but you're his mother, and there's no substitute for that."

"I know. He's all I've got left."

"No, baby. Now you've got me, too," she said, hugging me.

Chapter Seventeen

Candy

All I could think about was how I had let her get away. I had her, but somehow the bitch still managed to slip through my grasp. Or should I say slip through my gun sights? Eternity's traitorous ass hadn't been so fortunate, not living up to her name in the slightest, but that victory was short-lived considering that I was now in the back of a damn cop car on my way to jail for her murder. And Keyz had still gotten away.

Tears that wouldn't fall clouded my vision. Tears of rage and frustration, and tears of loss, because the reality of not raising my son, my future king, was settling heavy on my shoulders with each mile we traveled. I knew DJ was loved and Mona would take care of him, but she wasn't me. She wasn't his mother. But what kind of mother was I? I left my son to chase my sworn enemy, meaning I put my happiness, my satisfaction above what was best for him. What kind of mother does that? Maybe I didn't deserve my son. That didn't stop me from loving him and wanting to spend every moment with him.

If only Devaughn had never been shot and never left us. If only he'd come back. And whose fault was it that he got shot, anyway? Who had to fuck him again and again, becoming more brazen with my love for him and more reckless with how I displayed it? It was my fault. It was all my fault.

Now the tears did fall, and it was somehow poetic that I couldn't wipe them away any more than I could erase the destruction I'd caused in the past. There were no do-overs, only winners and losers. Damn, was I losing.

My pity party was interrupted by us pulling into the garage underneath the Fairfax County Adult Detention Center and me being roughly pulled from the back of the police car. They tended to dislike murders in this part of town.

"Got a live one," the cop said, walking me into the booking area and leading me to a big desk where a woman deputy was tapping away at the computer in front of her.

"Name?"

I didn't say anything.

"That's your cue, sunshine," the officer replied, smacking me upside my head, gaining him a look of hatred and disgust from me.

"Candace Wilson."

"Let's see. Candace Wilson, a.k.a. Candy, a.k.a. KD, thirty-one years old, no outstanding warrants, arrested and charged with murder fifteen years ago. Later acquitted."

"Oh, so this isn't your first time, then," the officer said, smirking as he led me to the fingerprint and picture station. I was quickly printed, mug shots were taken, and my booking was officially complete. "Hey, no worse than a pap smear," the same smart-ass officer said, making me yearn for my pistol all the more.

I was handcuffed to a chair, where I remained for a good two-and-a-half hours before my name was finally called to see a magistrate judge. All I could do was pray for a bond, any bond, so I could get back to my baby. Jail didn't worry me, but Keyz was back, and she meant to wreak havoc, and that did worry me.

"Candace Wilson," a female magistrate called, and I stepped forward with the help of my sidekick asshole cop. "What's the charge, officer Higgins?"

"Murder one, your honor."

"Facts of the incident and arrest?"

"At approximately 10:00 p.m. tonight, a security guard was doing his patrol out in Londontowne Estates when he heard gunfire being exchanged. He immediately called for police assistance and was told to wait for backup instead of proceeding in the direction of the shots. While he was waiting, he witnessed several people running, getting into cars, and fleeing the scene when a yet-unidentified female was hit with a shot in her right leg a few yards from his car. Before he was able to provide assistance, the defendant here ran down on the woman, placed a Colt .45 handgun with a unique type of bullet that explodes on contact to the victim's head, and pulled the trigger. The security guard was able to disarm and subdue Ms. Wilson, and now here we are," he concluded.

Now, I wasn't an expert on how these things worked, but shit sounded bad. Scratch that, it sounded like I was all the way fucked! I was going to prison, hopefully not for life, but shit, going to prison in Virginia was a death sentence either way, considering that Bloods ran the system. How hard would it be for Keyz to reach out and touch me? That only left one option. I had to get out.

"Ms. Wilson, do you understand the charge?"

"Yes, ma'am."

"And how do you plead?"

"Not guilty."

"Duly noted. I cannot set a bond on a charge such as this, Ms. Wilson. That will be up to the judge in the morning at your arraignment. Until then, you're a guest here, although I doubt you'll find us very hospitable."

Was this bitch trying to be funny? My response was to roll my eyes as I was led past the three men's drunk-tanks and put in one with about twenty females. Damn, did it stink in there! It was a seafood-lover's dream in this bitch, reminding me of how the popular seafood restaurant known as The Warth smelled when I was on my way into DC. Whoever it was smelling like that knew she was trifling, but I had other shit on my mind, like seeing the light of day as a free woman again.

I felt a lot of eyes on me as I made my way to the phone, and for the first time I realized that all I had on was a sports bra, my jeans, and some Air Force Ones that were pearl white, but now had red polka dots all over them. I must have looked like Thanksgiving to these hungry bitches, but I wasn't in no mood for the dumb shit. I tied my dreads together and then picked up the phone to dial out.

"Hey, slim, that's my jack right there."

"I'ma only be a minute," I said, not even turning around to see who made the comment. I got all the way to the last two digits of my home number before this bear paw of an excuse for a hand reached over my shoulder and hung up the phone. All I could do was shake my head, because I knew how this would play out.

As I turned around to face the crowd, I saw my fat, funny cop standing at the door, watching the action, but I knew he wouldn't break it up. This was his entertainment.

The woman who hung up the phone towered over me. My guess put her at an easy five-foot-ten and weighing 200 pounds, if I was being generous. I could smell her breath with her mouth closed, causing me to wonder briefly how many living teeth she still had in that muthafucka. Her eyes said she was a bully, but I knew that, so the way I saw it there wasn't any need for words. The smirk on her face told me she thought she had the advantage because she outweighed me and definitely had some homegirls in the crowd. The smirk on my face brought about some confusion. My advantage was that they hadn't bothered with a thorough search once they got me here.

I coughed gently, and she never saw the razor slip from my mouth to my hand, never saw my intentions until she was on the floor holding her ruined face, but by then I had ahold of the bitch who was next to her, and I was carving on her like I was Picasso. Like a wolf, or any predator, the scent of blood pushed me onward into the crowd, looking for the next frog who wanted to flunk biology, but everybody backed up.

My focus was so intense that I didn't hear the door clang open or the deputies storm in. I only felt the force of the mag light I was hit with as I dropped to my knees. The razor was slapped from my hand and my arms were bent at an impossible angle until my nose was one with the concrete floor. From there I was handcuffed, shackled, and dragged into the older part of the jail called the dungeon.

Not one officer said a word to me. They just threw me in a cell with all my shiny new jewelry on and left me to wonder if they'd come back before I pissed or shit on myself.

Aryanna

Chapter Eighteen

Ramona

I'd dreamed of him before, and if what I was seeing right now was a product of me nodding off, I knew I was going to be more hurt than I'd ever been. With so much going on, I needed it to be real. I needed my prayers to have been answered and my man given back to me. I knew I was asking a lot, but I needed two miracles to happen to me on the same day.

"Devaughn, is it? Am I? Are you really awake?"

"Your surprise tells me that I must have overslept by a lot," he replied, giving me that gorgeous smile that almost stopped my heart.

My tears came instantly then, and they flowed freely as I felt relief surge through my body unlike anything else I'd known before. He was real. My king had actually come out of his coma after five agonizing years, and here he sat before me, smiling like it hadn't been a day he'd missed.

I heard Deshana come in behind me somewhere, but I couldn't look at her. Even when I heard her body hit the ground, I couldn't look. I was so scared that if I blinked, I'd lose him, and I didn't think my mind or my heart could take that loss, not again.

"Baby, are you okay?" he asked, concern flooding his beautiful face.

No words came. No words would do, and so I threw myself into his arms and held him as tight as I dared. He was real. By sweet Jesus, he was real, and he was holding me again, which made me cry even harder as I buried my face in his neck. How did I begin to convey all I was feeling? How could I make him understand that nothing had been the same and could never be the same if I didn't have him right there with me? What words would do?

"It's okay, baby, you don't have to cry. None of you need to cry ever again when it comes to me, because I'm here."

I heard his declaration, but still my tears flowed. It seemed like my supply was endless, but I knew I needed to pull myself together, because there was so much he didn't know. "Devaughn, do you remember what happened?"

"I remember some things. Some things are like shadows at the end of my vision, though."

"You were shot," I told him, searching his eyes for any familiar flicks of recognition.

"Shot. Yeah, I was shot, but wait a minute. I can't be still bleeding, so why is there blood on me? Have you been shot?" His expression went from bewilderment, to concern, to anger, to cold-blooded murder. Oh yeah, he was definitely back.

"I can explain that."

"Explain ass, answer me!"

"I'm okay, baby. Stop getting upset and listen for a second."

"I'm listening, Ramona."

"Keyz shot me."

"Keyz shot you? Why would Keyz?"

Looking into his eyes was like watching a thunderclap, clouds shifting, and lightning touching the ground simultaneously. Not only was he back, but apparently his memory had now made the trip. Him being animated I could understand. Yelling, screaming, acting a fool, I could completely deal with that. But his silence? So much was said with his dead silence.

"How long have I been out?"

"Five years."

"Five–five years," he whispered in total disbelief.

"The longest five years of my damn life," I said, smiling and hoping to take some of the sting out of the moment. I couldn't begin to imagine the devastation he was feeling.

"So then, Candy?"

"Mommy's not here right now, Daddy. She had to get rid of the bad guys," DJ said, coming to stand in front of us.

I could tell for the first time that Devaughn really looked at him, then at La-La and Day-Day, who were just standing there crying quietly, and what he was feeling was plainly evident on his face. Love. Pure, unadulterated love. The love only a parent could have, and seeing it reflected in his eyes caused me to rub my stomach with a smile.

"So, you're my baby boy, huh?" he asked DJ, pulling him onto his lap with us.

"I'm not a baby, Daddy. I'm five already."

"And a big five you are. Anybody ever told you that you're handsome?"

"Well, mostly they tell me I look like you."

"Trust me, it's the same thing," he said, winking to DJs delight.

"I can't believe this. Ramona, why didn't you tell us?" La-La asked me, hurt and anger now taking the place of her disbelief and shock.

"I had my reasons, La-La, mainly being that I didn't want to get your hopes up."

"Didn't want to get our hopes up? He's our father. We deserved to have hope!"

"I understand you're mad."

"Mad? Mad? Ramona, for five years you let us believe our daddy was dead. For five fucking years. You watched our family fall apart, so I don't think mad even comes close to what I feel!"

"I—"

The banging on the front doors stopped my response. Only the cops knocked like that. "Shit!"

"What, Mona?"

"It's gotta be the cops by now. I'm surprised it took them this long, since Candy was arrested awhile."

"Wait a minute, Candy was arrested? For what?"

I felt DJ's eyes on me, and I realized too late that I'd said to damn much. My mind was going in a million different directions, and I was being careless with DJ's feelings, which is something I'd never been. "We'll talk about it later. Right now it's a big problem downstairs, and I'm not sure how to handle it."

"What is it?" he asked in that take-charge manner I remembered. Strange how my pussy got wet at the thought of the power of him. Well, maybe not strange, but sure as hell inconvenient since I couldn't get any of his good loving right now.

"We were attacked, and there's a lot of bodies down there, which is gonna require an explanation. A good one, too."

"Not really. It's more or less self explanatory, babe, because it was self-defense, and I'll vouch for that."

"You can't do that. You're dead, remember?"

"How could I forget that detail? Are any of the bodies Keyz?"

"Wishful thinking. Bitch has more lives than an alley cat."

"Mona, you said bitch," DJ said, trying to duck the lick he expected to come.

"Hey, don't talk like that, hear me?"

"Yes, Daddy," he replied, thoroughly chastised.

Again there was a pounding on the door, more impatient than the first series. I leaned over and kissed him softly, loving the feel of his lips against mine and the reunited dancing of our tongues. I gave him my heart, and he reciprocated, hypnotizing my mouth and putting my body under a spell of bliss that only he had the ability to cast. The whole time we were joined this way, we stared lovingly into each other's eyes, and I saw everything that made me yearn for him since the day he swaggered into my office. This man was my other half, and the sigh that escaped my lips as we parted was one of contentment and hope. My reason for hope was back.

"DJ, I want you to stay with your Daddy, and don't run off, okay?"

"Yes, Mona."

"Devaughn, I don't know if they're gonna search the house, so I'ma leave you and Deshana secured in here. Day-Day, I need you downstairs with me to give your version of what went down. I'll be back as soon as I can, baby," I told him, kissing him once more.

"No worries. I'll be waiting on you."

Reluctantly I got up from his lap, and with Sharday's support, I made my way back out of the library, only pausing when La-La caught us in the hallway.

"I'm still pissed at you, Mona, but I know you love him, and if you had reasons, they at least had to be better than okay. That's a discussion for later, though. Right now I'm both of y'all's attorney, so let's go get this out of the way."

"Thanks, La-La."

She smiled at me, and the three of us trooped down the stairs, where we found angry cops and flashing lights everywhere. As soon as I opened the door, they were inside, swarming like locusts.

"Ma'am, we've gotten reports of gunfire coming from this residence."

"Yes, officer, there are several injured parties, myself included," I replied, gesturing to my still-bleeding leg.

"Hey, Mac, get a unit over here. We got a GSW. Now, ma'am, my name is officer Sykes. Can you tell me what happened here tonight?"

I looked to La-La for the go-ahead and then proceeded to recount what happened to the best of my ability. All three of us were able to give varying accounts of the same incident without any major discrepancies, and given the fact that none of us had so much as a parking ticket, I could tell we were believed.

"Okay, so Ms. Petras, do any of you know who the perpetrators were, or who they work for?"

"No, sir, we don't."

This declaration was met with a stony look that had me thinking my previous assessment might have been premature.

"You don't?"

"No, officer."

"So armed men break in and shoot up your house, and you don't even have an educated guess as to who it might be?"

"I'm sorry, officer Sykes, is it? I believe my client answered that question the first time you asked it. Next question, please."

"Your client? You're a lawyer?"

"I am."

"Hmm. You do look familiar. You're Latavia Mitchell? That Latavia Mitchell?"

"I am."

"Okay. Well, do any of you know a Candace Wilson?"

"She's my girlfriend," I replied, my heart in my throat at the thought of what she might be going through right now.

"Well, then you know she's been booked for murder?"

"It was self-defense, officer Sykes."

"Not my call. So, does the name Kiara Briggs ring a bell?"

It was hard work keeping a straight face when just the sound of that bitch's name made my skin crawl and my heart harden. "No. Who is she?"

"Someone that was admitted to Fairfax Hospital with a gunshot wound. Maybe that's only a coincidence, but she'll be questioned when she wakes up. Well, an official report will be filed, and there will be more questions later, but for now it's best if you go to the hospital and get checked out, Ms. Petras. Ms.

Mitchell, you can come with us and give an official statement on record."

"Yes, it is. I'll have someone drive."

"Not necessary, ma'am. The ambulance outside will do just fine."

"Okay then. Day-Day, look after things while I'm gone, okay?" I asked, making sure she could read the message clearly in my eyes. I gave La-La a hug first, hoping to buy time or just a small window of opportunity.

"Hey, Sykes," another officer called, being my blessing in disguise as I quickly let go of La-La and grabbed Sharday.

"What the?" She quickly closed her mouth when she felt me slip the pistol from the front of her jeans.

"I'm going to the hospital, and hopefully everything will be taken care of properly."

She understood immediately what I meant, and I prayed Devaughn would, too. It needed to end. We needed to move on. And for that, Keyz had to die.

Chapter Nineteen

You Want War

Devaughn

Five years? How the fuck could I have been in a coma for five years? The little boy in my lap was proof, though. He was the spitting image of me at his age, right down to his dreads.

"Who did this to my hair?" I asked, reaching up and fondling one of my own dreads, another sure sign that a large amount of time had passed, because my last memory was that of a low-cut. Five years?

"Mommy did it, Daddy. She said she wanted us to have the same style."

"Uh-huh. And what else did your mommy say?"

"About what?"

"About me."

"She said that you're a good man and that you love both of us very, very much, and that one day you would wake up and tell me that yourself."

I felt the tears in my eyes, and my heart ached for him having to endure me being in a coma all this time, having to endure the uncertainty of what the next day would bring with regards to my life. My little man seemed to be okay both physically and emotionally, but I could only imagine the suffering Candy went through. And what about Ramona? How had she dealt with seeing a tiny version of me every day, knowing she and I might not ever get to experience that gift? So much pain... they all had been through so much pain. And it was because of Keyz.

"Your mommy was right, DJ, because I do love you."

"I love you too, Daddy. I told you that every day I came to see you. Don't you remember?"

"Of course I do," I lied, pulling him to me and hugging him tight. Some lies were okay to tell, and I didn't want my son knowing a moment's pain or disappointment from this moment.

"Daddy?"

"Huh?"

"You're squishing me," he mumbled into my chest, causing me to laugh and loosen my grip a little.

I had a son. It was mind-blowing, but he was real and in my arms, and he was mine. My son. "Hey, DJ?"

"Yeah, Dad?"

"What does DJ stand for?"

Looking up at me, his eyes shone bright with pride and love. "Devaughn Junior, Daddy. Mommy named me after you."

Of course she did. Candy loved me, and even after all this time I loved her. Looking at my son and thinking about his mother, I couldn't help but be grateful that Keyz shot me instead. She still had to pay for that, though.

"Who are you?" I asked the brown-skinned girl sitting on the floor with Lil' M's head in her lap.

"I'm JuJu, Deshana's friend."

"Her friend? Where did you all meet?"

"In Cali, where I'm from."

"Cali? What the hell was she doing on the west coast?"

"Daddy, you said—"

"I know what I said, DJ, and you better not say it. JuJu, what was she doing in California?"

"No disrespect, because I know you're her father, but you're gonna have to ask her."

The power of my stare should've been enough to change her mind, but Deshana wouldn't be running with a weak bitch. Maybe they were going together. Shit, who knew how much my daughter had changed in the last five years? I didn't get that vibe, though. JuJu was obviously protective, but not the way I'd associate with a lover.

"DJ, I want you to do something for me."

"Okay, Daddy."

I put my head to his ear and whispered my request. I had to do it twice, though, because when I said it the first time he looked at me like I was crazy.

"You sure, Dad?"

"It's okay just this one time, I promise."

He slid down off my lap and walking slowly across the room until he was standing in front of JuJu and Deshana. He looked back at me one more time and I nodded my head, trying not to let him see my smile. He paused for a minute, rubbing his little hand against his thigh, then he cocked back and *wham*! He slapped the hillbilly shit out of Deshana.

Quick as a blink, he was hauling ass back across the room, headed straight for me, and when he got close enough he made the leap into my lap. I was laughing so hard I had tears running down my face, and poor DJ was so scared I could feel his little heartbeat rattling his whole body.

"What the fuck? Bitch, did you just slap me?" I heard Deshana ask a startled JuJu. All JuJu could do was shake her head and point. The look in my daughter's eyes stopped the laughter in my throat as I saw the anger give way to confusion that morphed into shock until finally disbelief was all that remained. "It can't be," she whispered.

"It's me, Lil' M. I'm real, and I'm alive, I promise."

I watched her struggle to her feet and slowly make her way toward me, gripping JuJu's hand and dragging her along for the ride. As she got closer, I noticed the bandage on her shoulder and the dried blood that snaked scarlet trails down her arm. I felt my throat tighten, but I pushed the thought of tears back down and let the black rage that I knew so well simmer just beneath the surface. The bitch had shot me, my daughter, and my wife. She wouldn't get the chance to hurt anyone else I loved. I was gonna see to that.

Finally, Lil' M stood in front of me, looking the same as I remembered physically, except her eyes were older. The light of youth that I remembered was but a flicker now, extinguished by what untold horrors I didn't know. My baby wasn't a baby, yet she had a look in her eyes that I'd seen in myself on occasion. The beast had control of her now, and it was feeding on her soul, pushing her into that darkness I was all too familiar with. Could I save her? Or did I need to revert and become like her in order for us to save all that we held dear in this world?

Slowly, she raised her hand and held it in front of my face, just letting it hover as my breath danced on her palm. Her fingertips were soft and cool as she traced each feature of my face, remembering every line and indentation like she was reading brail or telling a fortune. "Daddy," she choked out on a sob.

Setting DJ down, I pulled her onto my lap like I had so many times, so many years ago, and I let her cry. I'd missed so much of her life from my twenty years in prison, then coming home only to find myself in a coma within the first few months I was out. She'd been cheated out of so much time with me, yet she loved me still in a way that was so beautiful and unconditional that it had me crying, too.

I loved my son beyond words, but this little woman in my arms would always be my first junior. She was my Little Me.

"Daddy."

"Shh, baby, it's alright. I know you've been through hell, but we're on the other side of it now. I'm back, I'm here, and I love you."

"I love you too, Daddy, so fucking much. I've been so lost without you, I–I didn't know what to do or who to be."

"It's okay, baby. It's okay," I said, stroking her back, motioning for Day-Day to come closer when I noticed she'd come into the room.

"Everything okay down there?"

"The bodies are gone and the crime scene techs just left," Day-Day replied, taking a seat in my lap.

"Are you okay?"

"It's just so crazy! I mean, you're here. You're really here. I thought, we thought we'd lost you forever this time."

I pulled my daughters closer to me, knowing no words could make up for all the time we'd lost or all the pain that came with it. I didn't have to imagine what they were feeling because I felt it, too. The incredible bond between parents and children is unique, but even more so when they've experienced so many hardships together. Our love was undeniable, unbreakable, but the cost of achieving a bond that sacred and tight was higher than we ever should've had to pay.

"Where're Mona and La-La?"

"Mona went to the hospital to get her leg taken care of, and La-La went to give a statement."

"Lil' M, why didn't you go to the hospital? Why did she hide you up here with me?"

Lifting what was left of her shirt, she wiped the tears from her eyes, then looked at all of us before she spoke. "Dad, there's a lot you don't know."

"Yeah, I figured that, but you can start filling me in."

This time her eyes fell squarely on DJ, and I understood that whatever needed to be discussed wasn't for his ears.

"Uh, Junior, I think it's about time for you to go to bed."

"But, Daddy!"

The look I turned on him stopped his protests before he could even switch gears. Smart boy.

"I'll take him to his room," JuJu offered.

"Give me a hug and kiss," I told him, scooting his sisters aside. After that was accomplished, he took the hand JuJu stuck out, and I heard him ask if she would lay down with him until he fell asleep. Smart boy, indeed.

"Alright Lil' M, what's shakin'? How about we start with why you were on the west coast and why you look like a smurf."

I saw the brief hesitation in her dark brown eyes, but she knew bullshitting me wasn't the way to go. "Well, I was in Cali because that's where I went to school. UCLA."

"Really?"

"Don't be surprised, Pop. You know I got your brains."

"No doubt. I was just thinking that you would've took over where I left off, because you were moving like a veteran in the streets."

"Be that as it may, I know how you feel about education, so I got mine. I actually just graduated."

"For real? What'd you major in?"

"Business with a minor in finance."

I smiled, knowing my baby had turned into an all-around hustla. "I'm proud of you, baby. That still doesn't explain why you're not at the hospital getting sewn up."

"Well, I don't exactly know. There might be a warrant out for my arrest." Her words felt like a wrecking ball being dropped on me. The last thing I wanted was for any of my kids to get caught up in the system, and even though I knew Deshana was in the streets because she got down with me, I'd still had hoped she'd avoid arrest. First Candy, now this.

"And what would you be wanted for?" Day-Day asked, ice in her tone.

"Sharday, don't start."

"I'm not starting, but obviously La-La will be the one to represent you. So, what did you do?"

I felt her whole body heave as she took a deep breath. "Have you seen the news today?"

"Care to be more specific, sis?"

"A shooting in Cali. At the Olive Garden in Long Beach."

The gasp that came from Day-Day, followed by the look of shock and horror was definite confirmation that she knew what she was referring to.

"Somebody want to fill me in?" I asked, knowing I wasn't gonna like the answer no matter who spoke it.

"Go ahead, you dumbass bitch. Tell Dad what you did," she said, shaking her head.

That hesitation was back in Deshana's eyes, but I hugged her to me to let her know it was okay. "There was this dude out there, kind of a big deal in certain circles. Well, he was a snitch, proven in black and white, and in exchange for a favor, I was asked to take care of him."

"Okay, that's not that bad."

"Let her finish," Day-Day growled through clenched teeth.

"Dad, you know we don't leave witnesses, so I shot who he was eating lunch with. The thing is, he was eating lunch with a police lieutenant."

"A what?" His forehead wrinkled.

"You heard me right, an LAPD police lieutenant."

"In California?"

"Uh-huh."

"Where they still have the death penalty?"

"Yeah."

"Oh. Fuck," I murmured, not even knowing where to begin grasping how serious this shit would be. A police lieutenant, though? And I thought I was a killer. Shit, this girl took the game to a whole different level.

Before I could speak again, it sounded like a gunshot went off in the little room as *wham!* Day-Day smacked fire out of

Deshana, who was struggling to break loose of the hold I had on her.

"Bitch, is you crazy hitting me like that?"

"You deserve it, with your stupid-ass!" she yelled, squaring up, ready to fight.

"Dad, let me go. I'm telling you, I'ma pluck her muthafuckin' feathers!"

"Cut that shit out. And Sharday, you better not hit her again."

Deshana settled down in my arms, but I could feel the tension in her body, and I knew to continue holding onto her. Day-Day just started pacing and shaking her head, obviously asking the same question we were all thinking. Who shoots a big-wig cop?

"Luckily for you, they are saying the Bloods are responsible," Day-Day said.

"How is that lucky for her?" I asked, looking from Lil' M to Day-Day.

"Because I'm assuming with the amount of blue her and her homegirl are rocking, they're Crippin' in full tilt."

"Crippin'? Ain't no way Lil' M would." But the more I thought about it, the more sense it made. Keyz was Blood and represented everything Lil' M hated, and since Lil' M was in the streets, what better way to feed that beast than to find a legitimate way to kill Bloods. All I could do was laugh.

"How is this all funny?" Day-Day demanded with her hands on her hips and her eyes spitting fire.

"Because your sister is not dumb, nor is she green to the streets. Crazy? Hell yeah, but far from stupid. She went in there disguised as a Blood to murder them niggas and have them investigating in vain. Dude that snitched was a Crip, huh?" I asked Lil' M, looking at her. Her smile said it all. "That must've been some favor you needed, baby, because that was a helluva risk you took."

"It was worth it." She didn't elaborate past that, and I didn't push, because I knew she'd tell me when or if the time was right.

"Day-Day, I want you to monitor that situation for me and let me or your sister know if anything changes."

"Whatever."

"First of all, don't *whatever* me like I don't deal with you, because I'm still your father, hear me? And secondly, we are a family, which means we take care of each other, no matter what. Is anything I just said hard for you to understand?"

"No."

"Good. Now, we need to deal with getting Candy out. What's the charge?"

"Murder."

"I'm sorry, you wanna repeat that?" I asked, hoping and praying what I heard was wrong. Unless I was mistaken, we were in the house Keyz bought, which meant Fairfax County, and a murder charge here was a death sentence.

"She's been booked on murder one. Sadly, the bitch she killed wasn't Keyz, just that traitorous bitch Eternity."

"Hold up. How did Eternity end up going with Keyz? She was as infatuated with me as most women we had running around this house."

"Do you remember the night you were shot, Dad?" Lil' M asked, giving me a look of concern and regret.

I searched my mind, willing it to travel back to a yesterday that was long ago for everyone, but a mere breath for me. The hot feel of the slugs ripping into my flesh was as real as the gun smoke filling my nostrils and the shots ringing in my ears. Still I pushed and probed deeper into my memory, past a sister trapped inside the madness of an unrequited love, further past a dead and disloyal man I considered a friend and mentor.

And then it made sense. I saw the blood on Deshana's hands and remembered sending her to kill Tara for running her mouth about me and Candy. Shaking my head, I looked to my daughter in my lap, and then to my other baby girl, finally realizing how much death and destruction I'd brought their way with my foolish decisions. How could I have been so blind to it before now? Did the grip of revenge have me so wrapped up that not even my child's embrace could bring me warmth? And if so, then what kind of man and father was I?

"I'm sorry. I'm so sorry for all I've put you girls through, because you didn't deserve any of it!"

"Dad."

"No, Deshana. I promised to be a father to you, a protector and provider, as well as a man you could look up to and be proud of. I've failed you in many ways, but I promise to make it right. Even if it takes my last breath, I'm gonna make it right."

I wasn't sure where the tears came from, but I felt them sliding down my face only to be caught by Lil' M's fingertips as she wiped my face and held on to me. Day-Day pushed her way into my arms until we were all huddled together, crying tears of sadness for our losses, tears of confusion because of life's uncertain future, but tears of joy at still having each other.

"I love you, Daddy," Day-Day said, squeezing me.

"Yeah, we love you, Dad," Lil' M chimed in. "Don't fuckin' die on us no more!" she added, hitting me in the chest.

"Trust me, that was not some planned shit, and I don't plan on going down this road again. I've been shot more times than 2 Pac!" I said, laughing to lighten up the mood. "Okay, look, we got a get Candy out of jail by any means. Fairfax is the wrong place for a body, and I spent twenty years in their system, so I know what she's looking at. Let's go get Ramona from the hospital. Lil' M, will JuJu stay with DJ?"

"Uh, Dad, there's something you should know," Day-Day said hesitantly.

Her tone of voice raised the hair on the back of my neck. I could hear a mixture of dread and fear, which meant I wasn't gonna like whatever it was she had to say. "What is it, Sharday?"

"Well, say Ramona went to the hospital to get sewn up because that is where Keyz is."

The five-year coma was having an effect on me now, because my mind was humming and buzzing faster than anything Microsoft manufactured. It wasn't rocket science. Ramona was gonna kill Keyz. But what if she got what she was trying to give?

Aryanna

Chapter Twenty

Keyz

Even with help, it was hard getting dressed. A lot of pain was blocked out by whatever dope they'd given me, but my whole body still hurt like a bitch! I was wincing in pain with each movement.

"Child, whose idea was these damn skinny jeans, anyway?" Gladys huffed in frustration, out of breath from the exertion of trying to get the jeans over my generous hips. I didn't know whose clothes I was squeezing into, all I did know and care about was getting the fuck out of dodge! It was time to regroup, because even through my drug-induced haze I could see my miscalculations and mistakes clearly. Intelligence over emotions was rule number one in this way of life. I'd fucked up by not only allowing my emotions to infect me and ultimately affect my decisions, but those of a girl.

"Thanks for the help, Ms. Gladys," I said, wiggling the rest of the way into the jeans and reaching for my shirt.

"You're welcome, baby. You probably want this, too?" she replied, handing me a Glock .40 that looked mean under the dim hospital lights in combination with the moon's reflection.

My left arm was useless, but the feeling of the rubber grip as my fingers caressed the double trigger lovingly was as sweet as my little boy's smile. Sometimes a person can only afford to be honest with themselves, and beneath the hurt, anger, and love lived a fear I'd never give words to. This used to be my home, my hometown, but now it felt like enemy territory in Iraq. This was war, and my mind needed to read it as such.

"Thank you," I said, tucking the pistol into my hoodie pocket and slipping my shoes on.

"Where will you stay, Kiara?"

"I've got a few places to hide. Don't worry, I know my way around the metropolitan."

"But do any of these places come equipped with a little boy that loves you with all his young heart?"

"I can't take him with."

"No, you can't, and I wasn't suggesting that in the slightest. Come to my house. No one will look for you there, and if they do, they'll get one hell of a surprise. That I can promise!"

Hiding in plain sight did hold a certain appeal, but Devaughn's mom's house? Really? That was a cocky-ass move, but I knew Candy and Ramona wouldn't dare attack me there, and so it was the best solution to a number of problems.

"Car's out back, Keyz, and the cops are distracted. It's time to move," one of my lieutenants reported, coming through the door while the other stood guard outside.

"I'm ready. Ms. Gladys, I accept your offer, and I will meet you there just as soon as I can establish my team around the city."

"Okay, baby. Come on, I'll help you out to the car in case them nosey-ass cops come back."

"Wipe everything down," I ordered as we crept out like thieves in the night. I hated the sight and smell of hospitals, which was why I kept doctors and surgeons on standby, but I was grateful these people had saved me. Better me than—

I never finished that thought because we rounded the corner heading for the stairs and I spotted a face in the corridor that froze my blood in equal parts of fear and hatred. I couldn't speak, but the comforting weight of the Glock in my grip gave me the strength to keep moving toward my goal of that stairway to freedom. I didn't think she'd start no shit right here in the middle of a public hospital, but no sooner had I thought it that my lieutenant's head exploded in front of me, showering me with his blood and brain matter. Even as he was falling, I couldn't believe that crazy bitch actually had the balls to shoot a muthafucka in front of everyone, but it was life or death, and the whys didn't matter.

Squeezing both triggers, I let my Glock speak, but I was thrown off balance by someone pushing me from behind. "What the fuck!" I screamed, sliding headfirst into the exit door, believing my second lieutenant had pushed me harder than necessary. But it wasn't him.

"Out the door!" Gladys yelled, still squeezing off rounds from the pearl-handled .40 DE. There was no time to argue, so once again I ran for my life. We scrambled down four flights of stairs and burst out into what should have been a moonlit night, but I felt immediate heat on my face and my eyes stung from the brightness of the flames dancing.

"What the? Is that my car?"

"Shame you weren't in it, huh?" he said, appearing from nowhere and sticking the gun to my temple.

Whatever drugs they'd given me upstairs had to be some next-level shit, because my mind was doing way more than playing tricks on me. I couldn't see his face, but the voice was so familiar that I knew every breath intimately. But it couldn't be! It was physically impossible, and I would know, because I pulled the fucking trigger myself!

"Dee?"

"Surprise, sis."

Aryanna

Chapter Twenty-One

Deshana

It was painful watching my daddy walk out the door, but the blessing was that he was actually able to walk. It was still surreal and unbelievable to me, yet somehow fitting, because he'd always been larger than life and twice as mean. I didn't want to leave his side, but it was time to get everything ready to finish what I came to accomplish. Having my dad back didn't erase all the pain and destruction Keyz had caused, and she had to pay the cost for her actions. Blood cried for blood, no exceptions or substitutions allowed.

"He's finally knocked out," JuJu said, coming back into the library.

"Good. I just wish he hadn't had to experience all the bullshit that went down, though. I have no doubt that he's as tough as our dad, but he deserves to keep that innocence a lot longer."

"Yeah, I feel you there. So are we gonna make sure that nothing like this happens again? I mean, that's my lil' bruh now, too."

That's what I loved most about JuJu: she was a loyal bitch, no matter the situation or odds. That was a hard quality to find in anyone these days, but my partner in crime had it in abundance, which told me that we'd no doubt own the game one day.

"My other sister just went to bring our troops out here, and my pops went after Ramona. After the homies get here, we begin strategizing our takeover, but in the meantime I've got unfinished business to tend to."

The look she gave me told me she understood exactly, so it wasn't surprising when she followed me to the elevator and down into the room where Jordyn lay strapped to a cold metal table. "I got this, Ju," I said, nodding toward a chair in the corner. Without a word, she posted up and began rolling a blunt.

"J-baby, you awake?" I whispered in her ear sweetly. My question was met with moans of extreme pain, and I could tell she was barely conscious. Her face was a swollen black, blue, and purple mixture, and her jaw was sitting at a sickening angle from its obvious break. "Are you in pain, sweetheart? You look like you're hurting a lot right now, but I promise it'll get better soon, okay?"

"Pl-pleasshh," she mumbled through swollen lips caked and smeared with blood.

"No begging, uh-huh, that's not allowed," I told her, stroking her hair lovingly. "You wanted to play this big-girl game. You thought aligning yourself with Keyz was your best move. So don't beg, because it will only piss me off more. Before we get down to business, though, I wanna enlighten you to a few facts you can take to hell with you. I did kill your dad, and you want to know why? Because he was a piece of shit that treated our mother like she was beneath him! Because he abused me in ways I'll never forget! Because he was an FBI informant, and a rat can't be trusted! But more than any of that, I killed his rich ass because he thought he was gonna kill my dad, and I couldn't allow that. You grew up with your father. I didn't, and I'll be damned if anyone robs me of that again. So," I continued while pulling out her beloved Ruger and putting it to her temple. "Close your eyes and picture reuniting with your dear daddy, because I've got a surprise, sis."

The sound of the doorbell chimes stopped me from pulling the trigger at that moment.

JuJu and I looked at each other, both asking the same question: who the fuck could be at the door now? "Come on," I told her, not worrying, but electing to be safe versus sorry.

We quickly made our way back to the main foyer of the house, and I signaled for her to wait while I checked the cameras. I saw no one. The only thing at the door was a small box with a bow on it, and I could just make out a cop car in the distance, driving away.

"No one out there, just a cop car leaving and a package at the door," I said, coming back to where JuJu stood.

"That don't sound threatening, but it don't sound right, either. I got your back," she replied, checking to make sure the .357 was loaded and ready.

Taking a deep breath, I opened the front door slowly with my gun out in front of me, and it was just how it looked on the camera. I quickly pulled the box into the house, unsure and confused about what it could possibly be.

"You gonna open it?" JuJu asked.

"Nah. Bring it to the panic room so I can roll the cameras back and see exactly what happened."

We made our way to the room under the stairs, and I pulled up the footage all the way back when the cop stepped out of the car. Pressing play, I felt unease creep over me as I noticed how familiar the cop walked as he carried the box to the door. I couldn't see his face, though.

And then I did. He turned directly toward the closest camera and smiled the sexy and brilliantly white smile that consumed so many of my memories the last four years.

"Trey."

"Huh?" JuJu asked, confused.

I couldn't utter another word. I just chanted silent prayers as I stumbled to the box he had set down. As soon as I opened it, my stomach heaved, and I felt myself sliding to a world of stars and darkness.

Aryanna

Chapter Twenty-Two

Ramona

The ride to the hospital seemed to take an amazingly long time. Or maybe it was simply my impatience to get there and kill that bitch. I could taste her death on my tongue like sweet red licorice and feel my blood pumping in anticipation.

"GSW, stabilized, ETA two minutes," I heard to the medics say over the radio. It was almost show time! I wanted and needed to play this smart, but my goal was simple: Keyz couldn't leave that hospital alive! She'd attacked my home, my family, and although I'd provoked her, I still knew that the lines of etiquette were too blurred for any resolution except death. Once she was dead, life could go back to how it was supposed to be, only it was now better than I'd imagined. The love of my life was awake, he found his way back to me after all these years, and that gave the future a light I couldn't describe. Plus we had our miracle, our baby girl that we would love, cherish, and raise together. Keyz was all that stood in our way. But not for long.

I could feel the ambulance slowing to a stop as we pulled into the ambulance loading zone, and my pulse quickened. The doors were flung open as the stretcher I was on was pulled out with the speed and expertise used to save lives. I scanned the ER as best I could while I was whisked in to have my wound cleaned and sewn. I barely felt the pain anymore. My mind and body were centered on one running thought: kill that bitch.

"I'm gonna give you something for your pain and discomfort, Ms. Mitchell," the doctor said, coming into the room reading my chart.

"No, Doc, I'm good on that. Is my baby okay?" I was trying to hide my fear behind my anger, but I was terrified all the shit that my body had gone through had jeopardized my daughter's health. I couldn't lose my baby girl, not after all I'd gone through to get her.

Rubbing my stomach, I wondered if Dee would understand that I loved, needed, and missed him so much that I had to have his baby. I had to! And it hadn't been easy, but medically it had been possible as long as I had the sample required for invitro. Getting that had been fun, considering I had no idea someone in a coma could still get hard and then get off.

Remembering my time spent with the man I loved brought a sudden smile to my face that only got wider as I envisioned our future. Late nights and early mornings!

"Your daughter is fine, and I believe you'll have a normal pregnancy in terms of risk. Try to avoid getting shot, though. I hear bullets are hazardous to your health," he replied, somewhat sarcastically.

A smartass remark was on the tip of my tongue, but I would have been talking to his back as he left my room.

I quickly got down off the table and began checking cubicles in search for Keyz. The Glock I took off Day-Day felt comforting in the small of my back, but I pulled it out and used my body to conceal it from prying eyes as I checked the rooms closest to the ER. It would take too long to find her like this, but I didn't wanna bring attention to myself by asking questions about another gunshot victim. Patience. I needed patience if I was gonna succeed in getting this done, but everyone knew that was the one thing no one can pray for.

And then there she was. For a moment I thought I'd simply conjured her in my mind, but her sneaky movements told me that she was real, and really trying to make an escape. "Oh, hell nah, bitch," I said, bringing the pistol up and squeezing off my first shot just as our eyes met.

The Glock was not what I normally shot with, but I still managed to hit the muthafucka next to her before she hit the floor for cover. Weaving through the crowded hallway, not caring who or what I hit as long as she died, I continued to squeeze off rounds in quick succession.

I was only ten feet away and closing fast. I could see her sprawled on the floor in front of the stairway exit. I could taste the sweet satisfaction of ending her miserable life!

And suddenly I was tasting my own blood. It filled my mouth before the echo of returning gunfire even reached my ears, and before I realized what was happening, I was on my back with my hands at my throat. I dropped my gun and put both hands over the hole in my neck, feeling my blood cascade through my fingers like so much running water.

"Get a doctor over here!" I heard someone scream, and then a nurse swam into my vision, looming over me. I couldn't make out her words. It all sounded like *whomp-whomp-whomp*, but I felt her hands strong, sturdy, and warm on my throat. I let my hands drop to my stomach, where I cradled my unborn child.

"My-my ba-baby. Save. Her," I mumbled into the bright light speeding toward me. But no one answered.

The light just went out.

***

Candy

It was hard to tell how long I'd been lying on the floor, but it was obviously long enough for my entire body to go numb. The shackles and handcuffs were biting mercilessly into my skin from where the police had tightened them beyond what was needed. It hurt, but the ache working its way around my heart hurt more. I understood all too well how bad this was looking for me, but my concern was centered around my son. He'd already lost his father to a coma, and now here he was getting ready to lose me in a way more cruel than that. Sure, I'd be able to visit with him, but to not leave with him, to not be able to love on him when he needed me, that was worse than death or a coma.

My thirst for vengeance had cost two lives, because me and my son were both lost now. Could this really be the end? Was this how shit had to play out? I knew my baby would be taken care of no matter what because Ramona loved him as much as I did. I knew materialistically he would never want for anything, but knowing these facts didn't ease my conscience in the slightest.

The loud sound of multiple footsteps approaching changed my course of thinking as I heard keys jingling with the guard's arrival. I knew cuttin' them bitches only made the situation worse, but it was eat or get ate in this world, and I damn sure wasn't on the menu!

The door clanged open, and before me stood the chick from the booking desk and a white boy that looked like a giant from down here. "He said you were a live one, but damn, slim, did you have to get it poppin' that fast?" she said, smirking.

I didn't respond. I just looked at them, wondering if the police brutality I heard about was about to become my reality.

"Grab her, six-foot-nine," she said, nodding toward the white boy.

"Muthafucka!"

"Calm down, shawty. We family, and I ain't gonna hurt you. Your old man is my homie. We did a bid together about twelve years back out in Tennessee. I'm up here because he needed a real muthafucka, a real Blood to look after his Ruby and your Blood drop, so just be easy," he replied, inching toward me and undoing my restraints.

I didn't see what choices I had as far as compliance went, and it was obvious he knew who I was. What I didn't understand was how he knew where I was, and how this broad fit into the equation.

"Can you walk?" she asked, scanning the halls. Looking for her coworkers, I assumed.

My limbs were numb, but leaning on the giant next to me, I was confident I'd make it. "Yeah."

"Okay, follow me, and do exactly as I tell you."

Once we exited the cell, we didn't go back the way they dragged me in, but deeper into the labyrinth that was the jail. I didn't look back, and as I regained more feeling in my limbs, I picked up the pace until I was damn near on top of her.

"Where we going?" I asked when we rounded another corner that led to a dead end with a door.

Neither of my companions uttered a word as we entered the door. Using her palm print, she opened the door with a silent whoosh of air, and I came face-to-face with the clear night sky and the noises of the city.

"What the?"

"No questions," six-foot-nine said, pushing me through the door to the open door of the idling Lincoln town car.

"Wait!" she called from behind, hurrying toward us with a phone outstretched in her hands. "Here. I've got a surprise for you, sis."

I took the phone and put it to my ear, not knowing what to expect. "Hel-hello?"

"You ever made love on one million in cash?"

The tears came instantly then, because I knew that voice, and there was only one man I'd ever said that to. "Is it you?" I asked, breathless, praying I wasn't screaming.

"Yes, baby. And I've got a better surprise for you," he said.

The screams were loud, long, and entirely feminine, which meant they belonged to one person only.

"Come home, baby. This plate of revenge is still hot enough for you."

Chapter Twenty-Three

Devaughn

It was so good to hear her voice and know that she was out of that jail. Now I just had to figure out where to hide her, because buying her escape didn't mean I'd bought her freedom. We were both wanted.

The ringing phone in my hand stopped my thoughts in mid-cycle, but on the whole I was feeling more confident about our life's outcome.

"Speak."

At first all I could make out was hysterical sobbing, which made ice of the blood in my veins. "Who is this?" I demanded.

"Mr. Mitchell, it's JuJu."

Deshana was my immediate thought, and I felt panic unlike any I'd ever known. "What's wrong? What's wrong with my daughter?"

"She. A box came to the house. The cops. But it was Trey."

"JuJu, stop! Form a complete sentence now!"

After a deep breath, her voice came back on the line laced with tears, sorrow, and so much pain. "Deshana's boyfriend dressed like a cop and delivered a box to the house."

At the mention of this, I heard my daughter wailing louder in the background, emitting a sound so heart wrenching my heart ceased to beat. "What was in it?" I heard myself ask softly, not wanting to know, but needing to understand.

"It was. It. La-La's head!"

Her statement was followed by a loud ringing in my ears. Then the line went dead.

To Be Continued…

A Gangster's Revenge 3
Coming Soon

Coming Soon From Lock Down Publications

RESTRAINING ORDER

By **CA$H & COFFEE**

GANGSTA CITY **II**

By **Teddy Duke**

BLOOD OF A BOSS **III**

By **Askari**

THE KING CARTEL **III**

By **Frank Gresham**

SHE DON'T DESERVE THE DICK

SILVER PLATTER HOE **III**

By **Reds Johnson**

BROOKLYN ON LOCK **III**

By **Sonovia Alexander**

THE STREETS BLEED MURDER **III**

By **Jerry Jackson**

CONFESSIONS OF A DOPEMAN'S DAUGHTER **III**

By **Rasstrina**

NEVER LOVE AGAIN **II**

WHAT ABOUT US **II**

By **Kim Kaye**

A GANGSTER'S REVENGE **III**

By **Aryanna**

GIVE ME THE REASON

By **Coco Amoure**

Aryanna

<u>Available Now</u>

LOVE KNOWS NO BOUNDARIES **I II & III**

By **Coffee**

SILVER PLATTER HOE **I & II**

HONEY DIPP **I & II**

CLOSED LEGS DON'T GET FED **I & II**

A BITCH NAMED KARMA

By **Reds Johnson**

A DANGEROUS LOVE **I, II, III, IV, V, VI, VII**

By **J Peach**

CUM FOR ME

An **LDP Erotica Collaboration**

A GANGSTER'S REVENGE

By **Aryanna**

WHAT ABOUT US

NEVER LOVE AGAIN

By **Kim Kaye**

THE KING CARTEL **I & II**

By **Frank Gresham**

BLOOD OF A BOSS **I & II**

By **Askari**

THE DEVIL WEARS TIMBS **I, II & III**

BURY ME A G **I II & III**

By **Tranay Adams**

THESE NIGGAS AIN'T LOYAL **I & II**

By **Nikki Tee**

THE STREETS BLEED MURDER **I & II**

By **Jerry Jackson**

DIRTY LICKS

By **Peter Mack**

THE ULTIMATE BETRAYAL

By **Phoenix**

BROOKLYN ON LOCK **I & II**

By **Sonovia Alexander**

SLEEPING IN HEAVEN, WAKING IN HELL **I, II & III**

By **Forever Redd**

DON'T FU#K WITH MY HEART **I & II**

By **Linnea**

BOSS'N UP **I & II**

By **Royal Nicole**

LOYALTY IS BLIND

By **Kenneth Chisholm**

<u>BOOKS BY LDP'S CEO, CA$H</u>

TRUST NO MAN

TRUST NO MAN 2

TRUST NO MAN 3

BONDED BY BLOOD

SHORTY GOT A THUG

A DIRTY SOUTH LOVE

THUGS CRY

THUGS CRY 2

TRUST NO BITCH

TRUST NO BITCH 2

TRUST NO BITCH 3

TIL MY CASKET DROPS

Coming Soon

TRUST NO BITCH (KIAM EYEZ' STORY)

THUGS CRY 3

BONDED BY BLOOD 2

RESTRANING ORDER

Aryanna

CPSIA information can be obtained
at www.ICGtesting.com
Printed in the USA
LVHW031540231121
704247LV00012B/1423